# I STILL SUCK AT TITLES

Ellen Taylor

# Contents

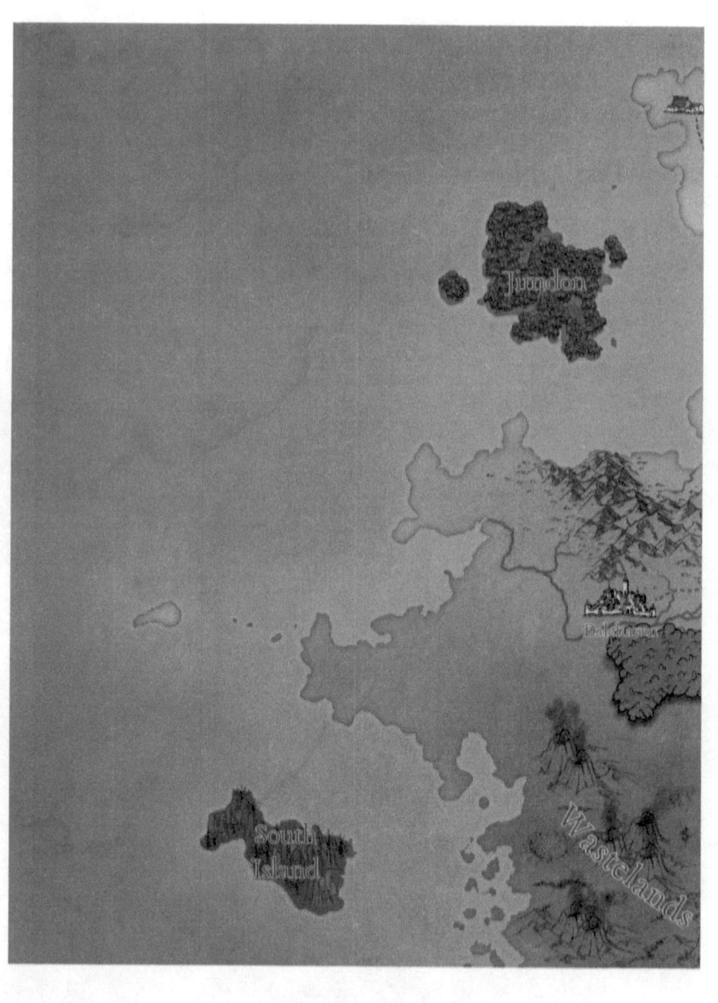

Jungdom
South Island
Dalehaven
Wastelands

To the Ice Lands
Omosa
King's Court
Vaywell
the Port City
Faerra
The Dark Forest

# Chapter One

# LIKE NO TIME HAD PASSED

Roger had the audacity to look confused. "Um, pardon?"

"Who are you?" I asked again. The only warmth in my voice came from barely contained rage.

Roger glanced at Paldric with.... possible genuine emotion of nerves. I didn't know. It was an uncomfortable reminder that I couldn't sense him because I never created him. "I'm Roger. I've heard a lot about you."

"That's actually your name?" I asked.

"It is."

"An odd name for Veniloria, isn't it? I'd say it's more common where I'm from."

Paldric's eyes darted between me and Roger. "Is he a G—"

"No." I gave Paldric the barest of glances before focusing on Roger again. "No, he's not. And it would be wise to not give such information to a complete stranger."

This mysterious character tried to get his hand back from my death grip. "I don't understand why you're so hung up on my name."

Hung up. A more modern phrase. My eyes narrowed.

**"Gunther, we're in the sequel now. I need you to write yourself out of your story."**

I'm busy, Devin.

Roger looked as though he regretted ever shaking hands, but I couldn't be sure since I didn't know his thoughts. "Can I have my hand back, please?"

I glared at this man not created by me. Once again, he used modern language. A person from Veniloria would ask for their hand to be released using ornate vocabulary. I tried to sense his code, to understand how he acted, but I only sensed two things from him. His name was Roger, and he felt an overwhelming desire to join Paldric's group. The Rogue hid the rest of it in an encrypted code I couldn't sense.

Oof. Roger and Rogue were too similar in spelling and might confuse readers. The device sorted itself out, already coding in the requirements to put in "Rogue Narrator" any time someone mentioned him. Which was great. Double the words every time. To make it even less confusing, I should figure out the Rogue Narrator's actual name to use instead. There's no way he can get away with any of this.

**"Oh, Gunther,"** Devin groaned.

Devin, hack into Roger's character file and tell me everything about him.

My main character seized my wrist so the character I did *not* create could wiggle free. Roger rubbed his hand, looking uncomfortable as I continued to glare at him. "Gunther? Can I have a word with you?" Paldric asked.

Panic gripped me as I turned my glare on Paldric. "'Have a word?' Did *he* teach you that phrase?"

"Um, yes." It was all he said, since my reaction to Roger alarmed him. Him I could read like... well, a book. He wanted to help ease me into the idea of Roger joining us.

"No," I said.

"It won't take long," Paldric said.

My scowl reverted to Roger. "No, he's not joining us. I don't trust him."

I kept my eyes on the Rogue Narrator's character, refusing to turn my back. It made it awkward when Paldric snatched my elbow and hauled me away. Once we hit a distance he considered safe, he faced me. "What's the matter with you? Where are your manners?"

Roger might read lips, so I barely moved mine. "I can't sense him. He's not someone I created."

"Didn't you create everyone?" Paldric's voice was not as quiet as I hoped.

"No. Not the necromancer or the Dark Wizard. Not the trolls, goblins, and shadow soldiers. And not Roger."

Realization dawned on Paldric's face, and he glanced behind him at the man who acted innocent enough. Since I felt nothing else but his desire to join our group, I refused to trust so easily.

"Maybe someone else created him? Not you, or the... the other one," Paldric said.

Once again, I redirected my stink eye from Roger to Paldric. The thought was, of course, absurd, but I couldn't explain why. I couldn't even explain that I was the narrator of his story and opted instead to portray myself as a sort of God. This story was supposed to be full of fantastical adventures of artifacts, journeys, and defeating dragons. However, since I arrived, I've been scrambling to make sure I'm not making any more of a mess than I already am. Someone (and my money was on the Rogue Narrator) snuck me a faulty narration device, causing me to stumble into my story. The Rogue Narrator, with his evil charac-ters hurting my story, was bad enough. No way another narrator logged in and created Roger and placed him in my story, too. Not without the Guardians knowing about it.

**"I'm checking that right now, in fact."** Devin's voice reverberated from the rafters above me.

The Rogue Narrator definitely created Roger, which means no one can—

Wait, we already know this about Devin's voice. And about the Rogue Narrator. Why am I repeating myself?

**"You're in a sequel, Gunther. The device will prompt you to reiterate important things to remind readers what's going on."**

I raised an eyebrow, then saw worry in Paldric's brown eyes. His shaggy, unkempt brown hair gave a taste of what we went through the past couple of days. Finding the shield and killing the dragon with the sword was enough that my characters deserved a weeklong party to forget the trauma of book one's ending. But now Roger appeared, and I refused to let my guard down.

Huh. Excellent summary.

**"In book one, you were incapable of writing yourself out of your story, but now you are in the sequel. It means a new narration device, and there's nothing stopping you from saying the code and getting out."**

Also an excellent summary, delivered by Devin, a distinguished member of the Guardians, and the man in charge of my case, making sure I got out safely from my device. That was a clunky sentence, but it worked. No one would read this book, anyway. I hated writing the beginning of sequels, just like I hated giving titles to my books.

Wait. Do I have to title this sequel?

**"Don't worry about it, Gunther."**

Oh good. Because I still suck at titles.

Devin sighed at something I couldn't understand before clearing his throat. **"This is your reminder that you are at fifty-two percent. Please say the code to leave your story."**

If I reached one hundred percent, I would realize how much of this world I could control. To do literally whatever I wanted with no consequences, and live out my wildest dreams as my body remained in a coma in the hospital.

**"No one doubts your summary skills. Now get out of the story."**

I could force Roger to reveal himself.

**"Say the code now. Please. Get out of the story."** The fear was obvious in his voice.

"Gunther?" Paldric asked. I looked at him again, a slight frown on my face. "You... didn't answer my question."

"Sorry. Zoned out there for a sec." Ignoring the apparent confusion on Paldric's face as I said extremely modern words, I looked back at Roger and straightened my glasses, the mistrust in my blue eyes. And brown hair. No, I didn't look at him with mistrusting brown hair. I just feel compelled to mention I have brown hair. Hair. It's brown. And blue eyes, in case anyone missed that. And glasses. Oh, and a bandage wrapped around my head because I fought and killed a dragon. It was epic.

Roger's eyes were dark brown with black hair that reached his chin. Honestly, everything about him screamed "secret villain that will absolutely stab you in the back while you sleep", even if he had an innocent enough face. For now.

"Gunther?" Paldric prompted again.

My smile tightened. "He can't join our group. I don't trust him."

Paldric grabbed my arm and moved me farther away from Roger. "A year ago, he and his wife went on a journey through the towns when goblins came out of nowhere and attacked them, killing her."

"He's just telling you a sob story to get you to like him."

I could almost see a hint of a glare as Paldric's face dropped. "He lost his wife a year ago. Show some compassion."

"Did he, though? Or was it just a story? I know the guy who created him, and he's always lying."

That was a tiny lie. The identity of the Rogue Narrator remained hidden, but any crazy hacker who entered other narrators' stories to mess them up is a villain in my book. Literally. And not the figurative literally. The man became my principal antagonist, ruining the last good thing going for me. I went through a messy divorce, living in my parents' basement, and now my story was in danger from the enemy of all narrators. Anyone created by the Rogue Narrator needed to stay ten miles away from anything I create. And here was Roger, trying to join the main cast of *my* characters.

**"You are at a dangerously high percentage, and cannot stay there. Remember, people who reach fifty percent don't last long in their story. You're a ticking time bomb."**

"I trust him, Gunther," Paldric said.

My heart rate quickened despite not being surprised that Paldric trusted Roger. Trusting people was his key characteristic, and one reason he was the main character. But instead of it being a strength, I saw it as a weakness.

**"Gunther, get out."**

The glare I pointed at Roger was permanently stuck to my face. Jim set this sequel up to require seventy thousand words, but it was still a lot. My story needed to end well for my characters so they could return to the database and live out their lives in an endless paradise. Once again, the Rogue Narrator stuck his characters where they didn't belong. Paldric would rally his friends to trust Roger. It wouldn't take much for Tara to trust Paldric. And Milla was only eight. Alwin might hesitate, but even he came to respect Paldric in the two weeks they traveled together. Future scenes tumbled into my mind. If I left the story, it wouldn't take long for Roger to gain everyone's trust. Then the Rogue Narrator would torture them for the next sixty thousand words to break them.

**"You don't know that."**

Why else would he create this guy? I couldn't return to the real world to watch a sadistic hacker crush the remaining hope in my life. The real world held nothing of importance to me.

Milla, my eight-year-old character, skipped to me. "Fifty-two percent."

In the code of my story, I sensed Devin altering the plot just enough to remind me why I needed to leave. Milla's ability was to help me know when my percentage was dangerous. The main reason I chose her was because she had big, innocent brown eyes to help me keep my humanity if I cracked. I stared at her, irked, which should have been a warning, but I mentally reached for the code instead. I inserted a few necessary things Devin never should've deleted, then eliminated a few crucial things from my safety net.

**"What? No! You can't delete the—"**

Devin was most likely demanding I turn the aspects of the code back on. The one we made before this entire journey began. He promised he'd never ask me to leave my story, and in exchange, the Guardians could shift the plot ever so slightly if I went past forty-five percent.

Milla combed her fingers through her sandy blonde hair as she watched me in concern. "Fifty-three percent."

I turned my scowl back to Roger. "Alright, Paldric. Let's make a wager."

My main character frowned, watching me. "What wager is that?"

"I'm going to stay until Roger shows his true allegiance. If you're right and he's harmless, I will apologize and leave this land at once."

"And if you're right?" Paldric asked.

Despite the spiders, shark, and dragon Milla saw us defeat, I still wanted to protect her innocence. I gave her the briefest of glances before leaning my head closer to Paldric's ear. "Then you better kill him before I do."

# Chapter Two

# INTRODUCTIONS

Paldric hesitated, then studied Roger again.

**"It's not worth risking your sanity. Put the safety net back, and let's talk about—"** The altered code cut Devin off.

I know you're trying to convince me to leave my story, but I can't right now. The Rogue Narrator will torture my characters if I leave, and I won't let him do it.

Paldric finally nodded. "I agree with your proposed wager." We shook on it before my far too trusting main character took Milla's hand to introduce her to Roger.

**"It's the Rogue Narrator or you."** Once again, Devin's voice took a serious turn. **"You will destroy your character's lives if you stay there. It doesn't matter how innocent Milla looks right now. You will do whatever you want with that little girl before you**

**make her cease to exist. I've seen too many stories following this same trap. Please, Gunther. Whatever torture the Rogue Narrator has planned, I guarantee you will do worse."**

Roger went down on one knee, smiling at Milla. My eyes narrowed, and my skin crawled when that man shook the hand of my eight-year-old character. If he harms her, Paldric really will have to kill him before I do.

**"Gunther, I must insist—"**

The code cut Devin off again. I folded my arms, leaning against the wall. Yes, I glared. The look was part of me now.

Tell me someone is working on cracking Roger's code.

The rafters remained silent above me. I briefly glanced at the ceiling, though it was pointless. Devin wasn't in the rafters. He was in the hospital in real life, speaking into the device over a headset.

Devin?

**"Jim and Grace are both on it, and Vince finds this recent development extremely displeasing."**

Agreed. Roger never should've gotten in here.

**"He's talking about your decision to stay. You've—"**

Devin once again got cut off mid-lecture. I doubted he'd end anytime soon, so I might as well introduce myself to

Roger. I strode forward as the Rogue Narrator's character got up.

"Hello." I tried to smile with my greeting, but it ended up darkening my glare.

"Gunther. Hello." Roger returned my barely there smile.

"I think we got off on the wrong foot."

Both Milla and Paldric frowned before looking at our feet, but Roger didn't look confused. Further proof his creator only used modern lingo.

"It's alright. We can try our introductions again," Roger said.

It hit me that the Rogue Narrator was listening to this conversation. He, too, would make sure his character acted how he should. Especially in the beginning. I stared at the Rogue Narrator's character before beginning my internal monologue.

You threatened my characters, Mr. Rogue Narrator. You almost killed them with trolls, goblins, and shadow soldiers. Pavaldri the dragon almost killed us, but I stopped you. You've been a menace to the Guardians for too long. Every character has a mark of their creator, and I will whittle Roger away until he lets slip who you are. I will not leave this story until you are stopped. I *will* be the one to unmask you.

Roger opened his mouth. "I'd like to see you try." My eyes narrowed. I *knew* it. Roger frowned, looking at me, Paldric, and Milla with what seemed to be genuine confusion. "Sorry. I don't... I don't understand why I said that."

My fingers closed around the hilt of Paldric's sword, pulling it partially out, ready to ram the blade through Roger's chest. Paldric grabbed my wrist. "Stop it!"

"He's evil! A servant of the Dark Wizard, sent to kill us all in our sleep! We must kill him first!"

**"Gunther, don't use any powers."**

I'm not! I just need to kill him.

"That wasn't proof!" Paldric said.

"It was proof enough for me!" I wrestled to get the sword unsheathed as Roger scrambled away, his eyes wide with terror. That look I could tell was genuine.

**"Your percentage is too high to decide life and death situations right now."**

Paldric forced my hand off the hilt before dragging me away again. "Were you seriously about to plunge a sword through Roger's gut in front of Milla?"

It was quiet enough in Lord Adrijian's dining hall for me to hear my animalistic breathing. Which was also when I remembered it wasn't just me, Paldric, Milla, and Roger in here. In my need to interrogate Roger as quickly as possible, I stumbled into the talking head syndrome. I didn't describe the magnificent dining hall fit for banquets in the port city of Vaywell, with large windows pointed toward the ocean. More importantly, I failed to mention the twenty odd servants watching horrified at what transpired. They should be scurrying back and forth from the kitchen to finish final preparations for a divine smelling lunch. Instead, they stared at my failed attempt to slaughter a man near their lunch tables.

This fifty percent was no joking manner.

**"You are quite correct. Please—"**

My eyes closed for the first time since Roger appeared in my story, trying to ease myself out of the anger. I needed to do better. My percentage was dangerously high, and I couldn't break. Devin was right. The mess I could make when I lost my sanity would be worse than whatever the Rogue Narrator planned. According to the stories, people didn't last long after they hit fifty percent.

**"Again, you should—"**

Get out of my story. I finished the lecture for Devin, because maybe if I did, he would drop it.

**"No, I won't! I'm deeply concerned!"**

Paldric finally let go of me. "Go take a walk. Cool your anger."

The thought of Roger out of my sight made my skin crawl, but if I stayed, my percentage would undoubtably climb. That couldn't happen, and I needed time to think.

Turning, I noticed the servants still watching me. My wave was pathetic. "Smells delicious!" That proved even more pathetic, but it sent the jolt they needed to keep setting up for lunch. I headed out of the dining hall but kept Roger always in sight. Which I did, since there were enough windows for that breathtaking oceanic view, as mentioned before. It was painfully obvious what I was doing, and Roger caught my gaze a few times as he talked with Paldric and the servants, but I didn't care. I was cooling down outside, but I wasn't an idiot. Roger was not allowed to hurt my characters. I'd make sure of it.

**"Are you familiar with self-fulfilling prophecies? Because you are literally setting yourself up to have your characters destroyed. If you don't want them to die horrible deaths, then—"** The device cut Devin off, but I got the message.

It was more painful to get hurt by a friend than an enemy. However, the fundamental difference between me and the Rogue Narrator was he actively wanted to torture my characters. Whereas I did everything in my power to protect them. If I left, I wouldn't have the mental capacity needed to watch them get so altered and twisted. This story couldn't be another addition to my failure portfolio.

"Hello again, Gunther," said a female voice.

Tara walked over to me, and I felt relieved to understand what she thought. True, being in Tara's presence was difficult ever since the incident where I understood too well how much power I possessed over a woman. It might never be fine between us, but it was still nice to see a familiar face.

"Hello, Tara."

Her brown hair fell around her shoulders in a way that wasn't perfect, and she didn't get too close. "I thought we could have Lord Adrijian and Lady Ana prepare a feast tonight before you leave. A way to celebrate you saving the port city of Vaywell and her people."

I winced, then looked into the dining hall again to make sure Roger wasn't going on a murder spree. Tara followed my gaze and frowned. "Who's that?"

Something shifted in her. My mouth fell open when I sensed the hidden code coming out. The Dark Wizard took Tara and tortured her while we were finding the shield back in book one. Tortured, meaning he tried to alter her character to get her to do what he wanted. It was my fault that Tara's character was undeveloped. I'm a straight male. I don't know how to write women. Let's just leave it at that.

With the insanity of the past day, I didn't think to have the Guardians comb through Tara's code. To check for anything left over from the Dark Wizard trying to alter her. But as Tara looked at Roger, a code I never sensed came into light.

Roger had an allure to him she couldn't understand. It made her want to find out about him. Possibly develop into "like." The "like" had the potential to develop further, and when I sensed that, I gasped, horrified.

"No! No! No! No! No! Nooooooo!"

Tara looked back at me, confused. "Pardon?"

I raised a finger, trying to organize my thoughts. I needed to explain to her I wouldn't allow us to stumble into the worst trope of a sequel. We couldn't do this. I hated this trope. It was cliché; it was trite; I avoided it at all costs. Yes, mainly because I couldn't write women, but I stood my ground. "Absolutely *no* love triangles."

# Chapter Three

# Not Only Am I Bad at Math, I Also Hate Triangles

After spending barely fifteen minutes with Roger, it was a delight to understand such genuine confusion on Tara's face. "What are you talking about?"

"You heard what I said. You love Paldric. Deeply. Remember that, okay?"

She took a tiny step back. "Right. I'll remember." Staying around me made her uncomfortable, especially when I said things that made little sense to her. All my characters assumed when my ramblings increased, so did my percentage.

"Come on, Tara. Correlation does not equal causation. It's the one thing I remember from my college statistics class. My percentage doesn't rise *every* time I babble. Just..." The example eluded me, but I was determined to find it, anyway. "Just..."

Tara's tiny step morphed into fully backing away. "I want to find Paldric now." She found the doorknob to the dining hall and hardly twisted it before stumbling through the door. Not that I blamed her. I terrified her, and she, more than anyone, knew how dangerous I could be.

Can you search through Tara's code, Devin? We should have done this earlier.

**"Not too much earlier, honestly. You've been unconscious for a day after your fight with the dragon. We didn't think to check Tara's code because we assumed you'd be—"**

The device again cut Devin off, and I never realized just how many times he lectured me about leaving my story. The random cuts in dialogue were starting to be more annoying than the lectures themselves.

A noise came from the rafters that almost sounded like Devin growling. **"Reinstate the original code, then."**

Despite my deep desire to continue this conversation with Devin (my duties as a narrator urge me to acknowledge he snorted at that) I said nothing, glued to the scene happening through the window. Tara joined Paldric's side before offering her hand to Roger. My eyes rolled as he took her hand and kissed it. He smiled up at her in a way she quite liked. I resisted the urge to bang on the glass to distract them.

The love triangle was worse than the miscommunication trope! I placed my forehead against the wall of the manor house and groaned. It was stupid. Cliché. The thing every mediocre sequel had for some idiotic purpose to keep readers invested. Oh, I hated this trope. Hated it!

**"According to the code, she doesn't have a deep bond with Roger yet, so if you deepen the bond between Paldric and Tara, the love triangle should never happen. Though you really ought to—"**

The altered code cut off the rest of Devin's speech as I groaned. The last time I worked on their romantic subplot, it ended with them too embarrassed to see each other for an hour. Granted, Tara was a better character now, but I don't work well under pressure.

**"Really? I never would've imagined."**

Shut up, Devin.

Tara giggled, and I glared as Roger finished some sort of joke. Tara already started giggling before the punchline. Once the punchline hit, Paldric guffawed.

My head hit against the wall of the manor house enough to vent my frustrations. Not this. Not a love triangle. *Anything* but a love triangle.

**"Again, just because she *likes* him doesn't mean she'll fall in love."** I glared at the sky, hoping Devin saw my face. **"Correlation does not equal causation, remember?"**

Another groan escaped me. Alright, I'll admit it. I failed statistics my first time. Good thing I didn't go to college to be an engineer.

Paldric and Tara needed to fall in love. Which shouldn't be hard. Except it was, because I'd messed it up already back in book one. Roger being here presented a writing duel. My knowledge of romantic tropes against what the Rogue Narrator knew. Even with the identity of the Rogue Narrator a secret, I hated my chances. Being divorced made me second guess my understanding of all things love and romance.

The Rogue Narrator wouldn't use a dragon to destroy my characters' lives. He'd just place a dark, brooding bad boy with a tragic past to steal Tara's heart. Science backed me up on this one. Women always went for the tragic, brooding bad boy.

**"You didn't go to college to become a scientist, either."**

Stop questioning my stem skills. They're not important to the plot.

I glared at Roger through the window again. Tried to sense anything from him as he talked with Paldric, gesturing toward the door which led deeper into the manor house. They headed over there, and my eyes narrowed, wondering what they were doing. Was Roger taking Paldric aside to murder him? Tie him up and drag him to South Island? Draw all of us out to the Dark Wizard's lair? Get slaughtered by all the cursed creatures?

They sat down at the table by the door. Oh. Lunch was ready. He wasn't gesturing toward the door at all. Roger wanted to sit with Paldric as they ate.

My eyes closed again as I rested my head against the wall, feeling the bandage still wrapped there. If I wasn't too careful, I could become incredibly obnoxious, so no one wanted to be around me anymore. That also could play into the Rogue Narrator's hands. Make me the enemy, so Roger seemed more trustworthy.

My internal monologue made Devin grunt, possibly in agreement.

"Gunther, are you coming for lunch?"

Ah, Alwin. My elf. The supportive friend and side character. The guy who lived almost a hundred and fifty years and watched three generations of Paldric's family. Our situation still rattled me, so I reached forward and ruffled Alwin's brown hair to hide the scars on his ears. His healing face definitely posed more of a distraction. Alwin frowned, confused. "What—"

"Don't tell Roger you're an elf," I said.

"Who's Roger?"

I placed my arm around his shoulder. "The guy who thinks he's joining our little group. He's won over Paldric to no one's surprise, and he might win over Tara. But we must be strong. You were always more skeptical than Paldric, so please use that now."

Alwin blinked a few times. His eyes were a hazel color. They were once so green they matched the forest, but he figured out a way to make them brown to further hide his elf nature. "I'm not nearly as skeptical as you."

"I know. Just monitor him, okay? I'm worried," I said.

"Worried about what?"

"I didn't create him."

Finally, after talking to all my adult main characters, I got the reaction I hoped for. Alwin glanced at Roger, the smallest frown on his face, the slightest mistrust drifting across his hazel eyes. "A minion of the Dark Wizard?"

"Possibly. I can't sense him like I sense everyone else. He likely has ties."

"I'll ponder what you said and keep my eye on him, but I also don't know the man. Perhaps there's another reason you cannot sense him." I didn't want to argue. What other reason was there besides the Rogue Narrator wanting to see me suffer? "Come, let's have lunch."

I followed Alwin into the dining hall.

**"Give us an hour, and we'll report everything we can about Roger. And if there's any leftover code in Tara."**

Until then, I was happy to figure things out the old-fashioned way. I sat across from Roger. "Hello again."

The shift was immediate. Roger smiled as he listened to something Paldric said, but once I sat down, he straightened his posture, his smile dropping, which was fine with me. He couldn't win my friendship that easily. Let him work for it. The only way he would get it is if, by some miracle, the Rogue Narrator didn't create him.

Alwin sat on the other side of me, and Roger's eyebrows shot up in alarm. "What happened to you?"

The necromancer had beaten Alwin, and after a day, his injuries were still healing. He wasn't bleeding, but his lips had multiple cuts scabbing over, as did his cheek. His broken nose had a bandage delicately wrapped around it, but at least the swelling around his eyes subsided. Despite all this, it took Alwin a moment to understand Roger's question because the wounds didn't bother him like they would a human.

"The necromancer. He tried to get me to do... something. And I didn't want to."

"I never asked you. Where do you live?" I asked in order to keep Roger from prodding further into the now deceased necromancer's motivations. Alwin's elf nature and my God-like powers were things I wanted to keep secret from Roger. Forever.

Tara sat on the other side of me, but I kept my focus. She wanted to sit by Roger, but Milla took the spot by him. Roger's eyes lingered on Tara before his gaze returned to me. "Now, or before?"

"Yes." I made sure he understood this was an interrogation.

"Here in Vaywell. I moved here after..." He trailed off, clearly wishing to keep secrets himself. Paldric watched me, his eyes narrow, his message clear. Roger wouldn't tell me about his wife because I would treat it with contempt. If Roger's backstory was fake, he did an excellent job squirming in his seat. Though maybe it was from the holes my gaze created in his skull. Metaphorical holes. My gaze didn't cause actual holes in his skull, even though I could. If I wanted to. But I wouldn't.

"Where were you before?" I asked.

"In Paerra. Do you know that town?"

My eyes narrowed to slits. Yes, I knew that town. The town right before Vaywell. In my original outline, Paerra was full of cheer and hospitality, but when we arrived in the altered outline, it burned to the ground. The destruction of King's Court was a devastating blow for the cheerful people, but what if Roger... "How long ago did your wife die?"

Roger's face dropped as Paldric's nostrils flared. "I told you that in confidence. You aren't treating this with proper respect."

The suspicious man across from me scratched at the tablecloth. "It's fine. It's been a year. I moved to Vaywell soon after her death."

He picked up his wineglass and sipped, not looking at anyone before placing it down again, trying to smile. It might have been genuine. Not knowing would drive me up a wall. Or cause me to crack.

To give him sympathy, Tara reached over to pat Roger's arm, but I grabbed her wrist before she could touch him and eased her hand away. Tara was at first confused before it morphed into annoyance. It surprised me, too. It was instinctual, that's all I could say.

The servants set down a delicious plate of steak and potatoes. In real life I was in a hospital, hooked up to an IV.

Despite not needing nourishment, my stomach groaned at the enticing smells, loud enough for Roger to hear.

"Yes, it smells delicious, doesn't it?" Roger said as though I vocalized my compliment.

I still glared at him while cutting into my steak. "So, you've heard, then, about what happened to Paerra?"

Roger picked up his utensils, not looking at me. "I did, yes." He sounded almost as pained about this as the tragedy of his wife. I just couldn't be certain. After spending two weeks understanding a person perfectly by looking at their face, this lack of knowledge felt impossible to handle. How would I ever survive the real world after this?

# Chapter Four

# DEVIN, JIM, AND GRACE CRACK THE CODE

After my short interrogation, Roger turned his attention to Alwin for the rest of lunch, ignoring me. I spent that time staring him down. Maybe I should have been nice. Compassionate, even. But the Rogue Narrator threatened my characters, and I wouldn't let that slide; not after what happened to us.

Despite my glaring, the steak tasted incredible. It was hard to show the enjoyment on my face because Roger needed to understand how much I distrusted him. Once lunch ended, Roger looked at me in a way I could only guess meant he acknowledged how long I had been glaring at him.

He stood up, which made me hastily stand up too. "Lunch was delicious, no?" he asked. All my characters agreed.

"Look, Roger, it was great to get to know you, but—" I froze. My eyes narrowed. I hadn't noticed it before because he was in the story and I was more focused on that, but as we stood across from each other, I realized he was a few inches taller than me. It didn't matter. Honestly, I wasn't insecure about it.

As I let myself understand this about him, I forgot I was going to say something, and we ended up standing in an awkward silence. Roger kept his mysterious, stoic look pointed toward me as he spoke. "Paldric? Could I have a word? Alone?"

"No," I said at the same time Paldric said, "Yes."

When Paldric turned his glare toward me, I blissfully understood it. At twenty-four years old, I was treating him like a child, and he hated it. Yes, I was getting possessive. So far, Roger had done nothing to hint at a secret assassin plot, and I couldn't force him to reveal himself if I was past fifty percent.

**"This gives us an opportunity to tell you what we've discovered about him, and if it makes you feel better, I believe your characters are safe for now,"** Devin said.

My gaze returned to Roger. "Fine." I meant it for both Roger and Devin. "See you gentlemen later. I'm leaving to... get some rest."

It took every ounce of strength to leave the dining hall first. I clung to the hope that I'd still know what Roger said to Paldric. Just studying my main character's face would give me what I needed, as long as he still showed up later.

**"The Rogue Narrator isn't controlling Roger. Not that we can tell,"** Devin said.

I need to be certain. Have you unlocked everything in his code?

**"Almost everything."**

That phrase didn't comfort me. It made me want to turn around and follow Paldric and Roger at a distance. I need to know everything, Devin. Roger's presence is dangerous.

**"Do not give in to the desire to control everything,"** Devin said.

**"This is Jim, logging in. Hello, Gunther."**

"Hi, Jim." I walked into my room. "Got your rest, I assume?"

**"I did, thank you. Looks like you did too."**

The bandages around my head felt itchy, as though waiting for Jim to acknowledge them before they became a nuisance. Paldric forced me into my sleep, but it worked.

Laws of medicine worked differently in stories. Knocking me out couldn't kill me. Books had their own kind of logic.

**"Is it true you made it so if someone mentions—"** The altered code cut Jim's sentence off, and I glanced at the ceiling, waiting. **"I guess that answers my question."**

After closing the door, I leaned against it, making sure I sensed no one near. With Roger talking to Paldric, no one could eavesdrop without my knowledge. I unwrapped the bandages around my head. "Before we discuss Roger, is there anything about Tara I should know? Did the Rogue Narrator do anything else to her?"

**"No, he didn't."** It was Grace. **"From what I gathered, Tara was incredibly resilient to what the Dark Wizard did. Liking Roger was not a danger to her, so she took the code."**

Once the bandages were off my head, I began rolling up the cloth. "This love triangle can't be the only thing about the sequel. Not only do I hate this trope, but the Rogue Narrator created Roger, and no happy ending comes from him."

**"After decades of experience being a woman, just because she likes him, doesn't mean they will fall in love."**

**"See? Grace is backing me up on this. There's nothing to worry about,"** Devin said.

I placed the cloth on the bedside table before tenderly touching the bump on my head. "As all of you like to remind me, where I am isn't real life. This absolutely is a story. The Rogue Narrator will treat it like one, and will get Roger to woo Tara."

The silence pressed between us. By not seeing anyone's faces, I couldn't tell if communication was happening outside my understanding. Despite meeting Devin and Jim face to face when I first arrived in the city to start this story, I honestly forgot what they looked like, and I never met Grace. They were voices in the sky I became familiar with.

**"Tara cares deeply. It's ingrained in her, even when she wasn't fully fleshed out,"** Grace said.

"She still needs some work." I paced throughout my room to keep myself focused.

**"But liking Roger is simply a part of her character now, because it fits. She cares about all the members of the group,"** Grace said.

"Not... not group. Roger isn't going to... he can't. Definitely not now. Not with that code. I won't allow it."

**"It's like I said, self-fulfilling prophecy. The more you force her to not care, the more she will,"** Devin said.

I took off my glasses and rubbed my nose. I didn't like this. Not at all. There was obvious danger to this entire thing, but Devin was right. The more I tried to control, the worse it would be. Strongly suggesting a better approach was the only solution.

**"Uh... you're still not getting it,"** Devin said.

**"Gunther knows his characters better than the Rogue Narrator, even if he read their personality codes. You can predict better than anyone what they might do,"** Grace said.

"I didn't develop Tara enough for me to predict what she'll do."

**"Oh, don't undersell your skills, Gunther. You know her better than you think,"** Grace said.

I tried to believe her.

**"Are you ready to talk about Roger? We know everything about him,"** Devin said.

**"Almost everything,"** Jim corrected.

I placed my glasses back on my nose. "Alright. Who's Roger?"

**"He was truthful about his wife dying. It happened a year ago, and he's still recovering from it,"** Devin said.

My pacing stopped. Two feelings warred within me. One of relief knowing Roger didn't lie. The other of realizing I was an insensitive jerk in the worst possible way.

**"He left Vaywell while I checked the city for any of the Rogue Narrator's characters a couple days ago. His depression got to a point where he felt compelled to leave the city to take a walk, as it was the anniversary of his wife's death,"** Jim said.

This didn't help the warring emotions inside me.

**"I know, but it's important. It means Roger doesn't have a direct link to the Rogue Narrator. It means he's his own character. Unlike the Dark Wizard."**

As much as I wanted to believe Jim, Roger threatening me after I gave my internal monologue was still too recent a memory.

**"Ah, yes, that's where we get to the mysterious part of his character. We think the Rogue Narrator placed a code into Roger, one we can't decipher,"** Grace said.

"And you didn't mention this at the beginning of our meeting because...?"

**"You asked about Tara instead,"** Grace said.

My fingers dug into my hair, and I winced at the bruises and cuts that revealed themselves from doing that. The bandage might have been better left on.

**"The best way to describe this is there's a section of his code acting like a USB port. Something in him is prepared to take another code, but the entirety of it is on a thumb drive, most likely in the Rogue Narrator's pocket. Whenever he needs it, he can plug it in and... well, we don't know. My guess is to use Roger like the Dark Wizard, since he recently threatened you with words that would only make sense as the Rogue Narrator,"** Jim said.

The anxiety I felt drove me back into pacing the length of my small room. "Did you see the code when Roger threatened me?"

Devin took over. **"By the time I pulled it up, it was already gone. I agree this situation concerns us. Roger brings a whole new set of problems we didn't expect, but if you—"**

As I waited for Devin to give up lecturing me, I went to my window, trying to spot Paldric and Roger.

**"What you've done is extremely dangerous,"** Grace said instead.

"I know." And yes, I did know. I was about to get into some serious internal monologuing that the Guardians would read despite me wanting to keep many thoughts to myself, but I couldn't help it. This entire situation was hard. I spent two weeks in my story doing everything I could to protect my characters from myself, mostly, because I couldn't leave. But now, given the opportunity to get out, I couldn't. Not only did I have to protect my characters from myself, but also Roger. The Rogue Narrator stuck his nose in my business and threatened to destroy my one good thing, both in this world and in the real one.

**"It can't be the only thing."** Jim's voice was kind. **"Come on, Gunther. Paldric gave you an incredible speech a couple days ago."**

"Yes, I know." My eyes scanned the grounds multiple times, but there was no sign of Paldric or Roger, and I tried not to be worried about it. "It helped me let go of the things I couldn't control. But this is different. This is something I can control. If I leave now, nothing will stop the Rogue Narrator from destroying my story." And I will have to sit and watch him torture my characters. Watch him try to break Paldric's optimism. Terrorize my characters so badly their essence will alter, and then they will no longer be who I created them to be. And at the end of the book, when they enter the vast database where all the characters of the different stories go, they won't enjoy their paradise. The trauma will be too much.

**"So, we're back to our plan from book one?"** Jim asked.

"Yes." I said it fast before the others suggested a different plan. "Once I hit the word count, I will leave. We will still have our dinner parties; still have relaxing moments away from anything that could tempt me to use my powers. Then when the book ends, and my characters enter the database, they'll remain true to themselves. Not only that, but the Rogue Narrator will never hurt them. And neither will I. They can happily live out forever in one big party."

**"You seriously think you can last another *seventy thousand words*? At *fifty-three percent!*"** The incredulousness was hard to miss in Devin's voice.

"Don't I have a nice chunk of words done already? What am I at now?" I asked.

**"You're at seven th—"**

Devin cut Jim off with a series of shushes and grunts. **"We need to put our safety net up first. Put the original code back, the one where we can—"**

I waited a few seconds to give my reply before realizing I wouldn't know if Devin had stopped talking, so I just gave my reply anyway. "And the code where you can fiddle with the plot if I'm over forty-five percent?"

**"You know why we need it."** He sounded exasperated. **"This is all for your safety."**

Devin's suggestion made me think. I considered all your advice, but I didn't dare do it. It was different back in book one when I hadn't reached forty-five percent, but now I had a feeling I'd never return to that number. Which meant the Guardians could arrange my plot throughout this last novel, which I didn't love. My goals didn't align with the Guardians, even though they were the good guys. From what I experienced already, I'd be listening to lectures about how I needed to leave every night.

**"Your safety will always be our top concern. You're already looking at years of therapy with Dr. Webb,"** Jim said.

**Who?**

**"Our top therapist, who specializes in unique situations with narration. You cannot—"**

Once again, I waited patiently for Devin to be done, as he had already proven my point by dissolving into another lecture.

**"He's concerned, Gunther. We all are. No one has lasted this long, and it's not worth celebrating. You cannot keep pushing your luck like this,"** Jim said.

"You're giving me two options. Either I leave now and watch my characters get tortured, or I stay, and you help keep me sane as I protect them. Between those two options, I've already made my choice. So, the choice is now yours. You either support me, or..." I had the threat I could use, but I doubt they would like it. And considering they could read my thoughts, there was no point in sounding threatening by trailing off. They might misread my hesitancy as insecurity, but if they weren't willing to support me, I'd just turn them off again and do this on my own. I'd use my God powers to figure out when I reached seventy thousand words, and then leave. As long as I wasn't insane.

It was no surprise when Jim jumped in first. **"Of course we'll help you."**

**"I will give whatever input I can on Tara, if you so wish. She's growing on me,"** Grace said.

There was a pause. Long enough, my gaze turned toward the ceiling. **"I'd still prefer a safety net in place,"** Devin grumbled.

I was coming around to the idea of putting it back when I hesitated. Something was happening outside. A loud something. "Hold that thought." I threw open the door and ran out of my room. I tried not to think of the worst-case scenario, but I was still painfully aware Roger went on a walk alone with Paldric.

# Chapter Five

## KILLING THE MESSENGER

It was worse. Guards spilled out of the manor house, shouting commands as they left. My heart stilled as I sprinted outside, watching the organized chaos. Guards crowded the streets, prepared for a fight. A dozen women with their bows and arrows hurried toward the magnificent archway that travelers always saw when coming into Vaywell. The archway was intricately carved, and a source of pride for Vaywell. It was, indeed, beautiful, but I would have rather had a stone wall around the city, considering the circumstances.

Goblins. Two hundred of them outside the city. If I closed my eyes and concentrated, I heard them screaming as the sunlight fueled their berserker rage with a desire to make Vaywell burn.

"Gunther!" Tara held her skirts to make it easier to dash toward me. "Where's Paldric?"

My eyes closed, probing for my main character. Paldric's desire to help was easiest to sense as he sprinted for the archway of the city. Alwin was already there, dropping goblins with his bow and arrow.

"Heading toward the archway. Him and Alwin. They're trying to help."

"And Roger?"

If I couldn't sense his character, then I wouldn't be able to know where he was, but I tried all the same before opening my eyes. "I don't know." Admitting it out loud hurt. Roger could be anywhere. Either helping my characters or pushing them toward the goblins. With that thought, I ran toward the archway. Tara raced after me.

**"It's not in his character's code. He won't do it,"** Jim said.

Unless the Rogue Narrator inserted the code already.

**"We'd have seen it if he did. It's not there,"** Devin said.

Makes little difference. It could appear any time. Wait, can you read what the goblin code is?

**"Yes. These goblins aren't here to conquer Vaywell. They're here to scare the inhabitants and..."** Grace paused, most likely reading the code as it appeared. **"And make sure they deliver a message."**

My pace quickened once we passed the archway. "Tara, go back and stay with Milla."

She kept up with me, out of breath, but it didn't stop her from speaking. "Lady Ana is protecting Milla. They might need a healer out here." Tara was becoming her own character, and I would rather have her disagree and get angry at me than obey my every demand. Though sometimes I wished she would listen to me. Like if I told her Roger was horrible for her. That would be nice.

**"Don't force it, Gunther,"** Devin said.

We followed the surge of guards and men.

**"You passed the messenger. Go back. Then left a few more paces,"** Grace said. Near the archway, two guards held an unconscious third man, dragging him away from the battle. **"That's him. That's the message they want to send you."**

The tension in my shoulders relaxed when I didn't recognize the unconscious man, then instantly felt bad about it. When Grace said there was a message, I feared someone would drag Paldric in with an arrow sticking out of his chest. Yes, this man's condition concerned me. He was a filler character programed to stand guard, but he was still mine.

Tara pushed past me, her pack in her hands. "I have supplies and am trained as a healer."

The two guards nodded, easing the unconscious man next to the archway as the battle surged forward. The second the man was on the ground, Tara got to work. I winced as she pulled back his shirt to reveal his injuries. Deep claw marks covered his chest, which only a goblin could produce. The man barely breathed. The longer I stared at his face, the more certain I became of his passing.

I knelt next to him across from Tara, uncertain he would ever wake up, and felt useless despite being the narrator of the story. Tara began cleaning his wounds, mumbling orders to the guards to hold bits of cloth where she needed. She wrapped the cuts, staying calm for the patient, even if he was almost dead.

Too afraid to touch him in case it caused more pain, I set my hand next to him and closed my eyes, sensing the character I created. It came to me how he got the injuries. The goblins appeared at Dalehaven, where this man lived, overwhelming the city. It was the first city a person would arrive at if, say, they traveled from South Island.

His sputtering brought me to the present. The man labored to peel his eyes open. "He's cast the spell. South Island..."

Through his mind, I saw dark light shoot into the sky a few days before. A week ago, the Dark Wizard and the necromancer used my reanimated dragon to gather the final ingredients. Then he created the bridge, linking South Island to Veniloria.

"He found the armor... women and children fled... those who didn't... who stood against him... were slaughtered..."

Despite forcing myself to not react, fear trickled through my eyes right as Tara caught my gaze. She stared long enough to acknowledge the emotion before resuming her work of cleaning wounds.

Dalehaven was gone. Ransacked by cursed creatures. I thought of all the warrior characters I had spent creating. Petari and Elia. Rejhio would definitely never flee. Even the nameless innkeeper with a missing leg would be gone now. If the warrior city couldn't handle the cursed creatures, what could Vaywell do?

Past the archway, the battlefield was slick with the goblin's purple blood. Two hundred wouldn't break Vaywell, but a thousand could. Especially if that thousand also had trolls and shadow soldiers with them. The Dark Wizard clearly didn't care if we killed this little army of two hundred goblins, because more was coming. A lot more.

A goblin snarled as it crawled through the grass, heading straight for us. The grimy black hair, in contrast with its slimy pale skin, was enough to stop my heart. It could have been as tall as a man if the creature's back wasn't broken in multiple places and magically put together again. The fact that his legs were missing also didn't help with his height.

One guard hastily got to his feet and stabbed the goblin, waiting long enough to confirm it was dead. The other guard placed a hand over Tara's, stopping her from cleaning the wound. "You don't need to continue. The man has passed. Save your supplies."

Tears leapt to her eyes as she studied the dead man's face. She did everything she could, but his injuries were too deep. This secret was the only reason the goblins didn't kill him. Goblins killed everything while in the sunlight, so it must have taken quite the mental battle to fight against their desire. They had orders, and they wouldn't disobey their master.

"Where's Alwin?" Even though I directed my question to the Guardians, I asked it out loud. Too much was happening, and I needed to find him now.

"What?" Tara asked.

**"Getting surrounded on the southern side of the battle,"** Jim said.

Grabbing the dead goblin's sword, I scrambled to my feet. Tara, used to my oddities, remained with the guards and said nothing, preparing to heal more soldiers.

I hate admitting this to you, of all people, Jim, but I don't understand cardinal directions. Just guide me there.

**"What? Why don't you want to admit this to me?"**

Because you have a perfect life. And of course you know cardinal directions.

Jim sighed. **"I doubt you'll believe me when I say my life isn't perfect, but first let's save your elf. Go past the archway."**

Trepidation filled my stomach as I ran. With the Rogue Narrator draining South Island, my elf became the most important person in Veniloria. The goblins would drag him to the Dark Wizard to force him to activate the armor using whatever means necessary.

**"Go left again, straight through those goblins."**

I sprinted through, cutting whatever goblin tried to get in my way.

**"Yeah, that was my bad. I didn't necessarily mean for you to go straight through those goblins, just that Alwin was past this small gathering,"** Jim said.

Too late now. Past this army, I noticed the cluster of goblins. With a sinking gut, I sensed who was in the middle of it.

**"Yep,"** Jim said.

Which was when my traitorous self-doubt reminded me I had zero sword skills. True, goblins didn't either, but they raged in the sunlight, hacking at whatever they could, so I did, too. The recent memory of a legless goblin attempting to kill us drove my desire to leave none of their head still attached.

It took four felled goblins before their neighbors turned, acknowledging me as a threat. One of them kicked me hard in the chest and I went soaring, right into the pointed end of another goblin's staff, which would have skewered me if my invulnerability didn't kick in. I dropped to the ground, perfectly fine. The goblins, despite their rage, noticed this fresh development.

Devin groaned. **"Not good. They found the man who would burn the world, so according to their master, they must make you crack."**

Well, that was dramatic, Devin. Are you a narrator or something?

**"Ha ha."** There was zero mirth in his laugh.

Fine, I just needed to improvise. The goblin sword slid in my sweaty palms as I scrambled to my feet. "Oh, ouch. That hurt so bad. I'm bleeding out now. It's just... impossible to see the blood. Because... it matches the color of the ground."

The goblins sneered.

**"Get out of there, Gunther,"** Devin said.

I hardly had time to breathe before the goblin horde descended on me. There was no way I could run. Despite my invulnerability and being two weeks into my story, my knee jerk instinct hit when I saw twenty swords and sharpened staffs headed straight for me. I dropped back to the ground, curled up into myself, and braced for pain as Devin sighed in the skies above.

The pain never happened. Sure, I felt the swords hitting me, but the pain wasn't there. It felt like a lot of pillows aimed at my head.

I didn't think I was cracking, but being over fifty percent and charging into a battle with nothing more than an idea to save Alwin certainly didn't help. They kicked the goblin sword out of my hands, which made it easier to curl into myself.

The goblins shouted to their fellows.

"God is here!"

"Needs to crack!"

"Help us crack him!"

And just like that, the rest of the goblins came after me with their swords held high. On a positive note, with the horde focused on cracking me, the army could easily cut them down. All I had to do was wait.

Their swords, attempting to chop me into stew, kept me curled on the ground. I covered my face, a thick layer of dust settling on me. My lungs sucked in the dust covered air to distract myself from how I could force them all to drop with a thought. When the sunlight hit my face, I lowered my hands to see Roger finishing the last goblin. He turned to me, his sword dripping with purple blood. His stoicism gave way to surprise when he saw me still breathing.

How was I supposed to explain this to *him*?

# Chapter Six

# I Learn More Unsettling Truths About Roger

"Hello, Roger." I spoke into my hands, still curled into a ball in the dirt. If I stayed like this long enough, maybe everyone will consider it normal behavior. Come to think of it, perhaps everyone in Vaywell thought I was the bee's knees for killing a dragon. I could start a trend. Curling up on the ground. Covered in dust. After being surrounded by goblins.

Roger stared at me with wide eyes and a slack jaw. "How are you still alive?"

The words tumbled from my mouth before I could stop them. "Family secret."

He extended his hand to me, which I begrudgingly took. After he helped pull me to my feet, I brushed the thick layer of dirt from my clothes. Roger studied me, then examined the fifty goblins lying dead around us. "The goblins called you a God?"

My brushing slowed, then I straightened to meet Roger's gaze, realizing with a sinking heart he might actually be taller than me. Not like it mattered. I wasn't intimidated. He wasn't *that* much taller. I looked around the battlefield to distract myself. Men weaved through the bodies, searching for injured. "Yeah. They did."

"Are you?" Roger asked.

"Do I look like a God?"

It was a good non-answer, because it satisfied Roger. My eyes fell on Alwin, who was cleaning his sword. I ignored Roger and headed straight for my elf. Rude? Without a doubt. But I wanted to postpone this conversation for as long as possible.

"Alwin? Are you alright?" I asked.

"Fine." He didn't look at me as he finished cleaning his sword. Despite his injuries from the Dark Wizard, I couldn't sense any new ones. Alwin glanced at Roger, an elf frown appearing on his face as he sheathed his sword. He pushed past me and headed straight for Roger before I noticed him tenderly holding his side. "Roger?"

"Just a minor cut. I'll be fine." Alwin lifted Roger's hand from his side and saw it covered in blood. My eyes widened. He expertly hid an injury from me because I couldn't sense his hurt.

Despite everything, I winced when I saw it, then a fresh horror gripped me. It already played before my mind. We take Roger to Tara. He takes off his shirt. They do the same thing she and Paldric did to create a bond in book one.

I went to the other side of Roger, taking his arm. My eyes scanned the battlefield until I found a filler character who was an old soldier. "Over here."

"Gunther, what—" Roger started to say.

"It's no trouble. You're really not that tall. I can manage," I said.

"Not that..." Roger took a moment to check my height. "It doesn't really matter."

"Nope. It doesn't. It absolutely doesn't," I said.

The filler character looked surprised as he saw us approach. "Hello, can I help you?"

Alwin and Roger were confused, so they said nothing, which gave me the opportunity to speak without being interrupted. "It's within reason that all soldiers would have a basic understanding of healing services, right?"

The filler character frowned, but I sensed the code entering all soldiers. "It would make sense, yes." This wouldn't use any of my God powers, because as narrator, I did this stuff all the time. Which... okay, maybe I'd have to double check my percentage.

**"Always err on the side of checking your percentage,"** Devin said.

"It also makes sense that you would have a large encyclopedic knowledge of healing techniques. Since you've gotten plenty of experience on the battlefield."

The filler character may not have understood all my words, but he still nodded as this entered his code. "It would, yes, sir."

I motioned to Roger with my free hand. "And therefore, it would be easy to clean a wound such as this, since carrying him into the city will take too long."

The man's eyes traveled to Roger's wound and lifted his shirt enough to examine it with expert eyes. He took the small bundle of healing supplies Alwin offered him. "Nasty, no doubt, but not deep. Set him down, gentlemen. I'll get him on his feet soon."

We obeyed, then I patted the gentleman on the shoulder. "Thank you, good man."

My filler character got to work. I stood, searching the battlefield for any sign of Paldric. Despite my fear for Alwin's safety, my main character still concerned me, too.

"You two go ahead. I'll be fine," Roger said.

I nodded, moving toward the city, sensing the code. Paldric was alive and well, with barely any injuries.

"Is there a reason you act so cold around Roger?" Alwin asked once we were far enough away that Roger couldn't overhear.

"I don't trust him," I said.

"He helped save your life."

"I'm invulnerable. My life doesn't need saving."

Alwin glanced back to see the filler character working fast on Roger's wound. "He didn't know that. He risked his life for you and got a nasty cut. The least you could do is show some gratitude."

**"Alwin has a point, you know,"** Devin said.

He's still got a hidden code I cannot trust. The Rogue Narrator himself put it in there. I can't drop my guard around him.

**"But you don't have to treat him coldly."**

I glanced behind me to see Roger on the ground with the old soldier. The look on Roger's face when he saw me curled into a ball returned to mind. He was surprised, yet compassionate. And the way I didn't realize how hurt he was? Yep, I was being more than cold. This was borderline cruel.

And yet there was that unknown factor I couldn't shake. Once the Rogue Narrator gave the word, Roger could kill all my characters.

**"You don't know that, dear. The code doesn't say he'll turn into a merciless killer,"** Grace said.

My response to Grace was well thought out until I saw Paldric walk over to us, limping noticeably with a swollen foot. "Paldric, get off your foot."

"Just a sprain. I'll be fine."

He resisted, but I still grabbed his arm and threw it over my shoulder to help him get the weight off. "Get off it so it won't become worse. We've had a recent development." I told them about the message from the dying filler character as we left the battlefield. I didn't actually say 'filler character', because that would have raised questions I couldn't answer.

Once we passed the archway and got into Vaywell, I finished relaying the message. Alwin met my eyes, and I sensed his fear. My elf understood almost as much as me the Dark Wizard's ambition to tear this world apart to activate the artifacts. In fact, Alwin already planned how to slip away so no one could find him, not even me. "Don't even try it."

My elf didn't bother asking how I knew his thoughts. Instead, he gave a human-like shrug. "It would be safer."

"And the Dark Wizard would still tear Veniloria apart to find you. He will burn down forests or kidnap us to draw you out. Our best bet is to stick together."

Despite the pain he struggled to hide, Paldric moved his head to give me a curious look. "Including Roger?"

My hesitation was long enough that both my characters showed their disapproving expressions. We slipped through the injured men being tended to. Several healers were out, cleaning and wrapping wounds. Thankfully, this battle did not cause too many horrible injuries.

I dropped my voice so my filler characters couldn't hear. "You realize I didn't create him, right? Having him with us guarantees the enemy knows where we are."

"You don't know he—" Paldric started to say.

"Yes, I do. And he is." Paldric shook his head, limping along because he *still* wasn't listening to me. "Stop walking on your foot."

Tara ran to us, terrified because I held Paldric in a way that clearly meant he was dying.

"It's nothing," Paldric said as Tara knelt to inspect his foot. "Really, a small bruising on my ankle."

"I'll check it all the same. Come sit." Tara took Paldric's other arm and helped him to a small stone fountain. It had nymphs and fairies dancing around a tree that sprouted water, impossibly made considering I set this in a medieval time period.

Tears pricked Tara's eyes, and she didn't hide them. The more I studied her, the more I realized why. Grace was right. Tara did care, deeply. She wasn't a war healer. The small town she lived in dealt with bumps, bruises, and maybe some broken bones or hunting accidents. War wounds of this magnitude made her slip into a quiet alleyway to steady her nerves, going through stories of her mother. It was what her father suggested when she was little. When the heartache of a failed healing affected her mental state too much. This entire battle shook her, especially the memory of the man dying as she tried to heal him. Even though they met briefly, she shed a few tears for a man she couldn't save, and I almost felt bad referring to him purely as a filler character.

Tara wrapped Paldric's foot as tightly as possible, saying it was a bad bruising, but it could get better if he'd stay off it. Paldric had every intention of obeying Tara, despite me telling him the same thing.

"What do we do now?" Paldric asked.

They all turned to me, and I hated it. Book two needed to be boring. We needed to attend parties, have feasts, not do anything that would tempt me to use my powers. Suggest strongly that Paldric and Tara create a relationship so she wouldn't run to Roger instead. Narrating my least favorite trope was now enviable compared to what the Rogue Narrator had in mind.

Every inhabitant of South Island was headed straight for us. The Dark Wizard had, as far as I could tell, two objectives. Kidnap Alwin to activate the armor, and harm my characters so I would crack. I needed to survive seventy-thousand words. Hopefully less, now.

Milla ran up to me. "You're at fifty-three percent."

"Really?" I was genuinely surprised. "That entire battle and I didn't raise one percent? After using my invulnerability for so long?"

"It raised your percentage a little, even though you did nothing but take it. But making a fool of yourself in front of Roger let it drop it back down. I don't know what that means, but there you go."

Paldric, Alwin, and Tara all looked at me, curious about what Milla meant.

"What? No... I didn't... that's not what..."

"I heard my name. Can I help in any way?" Roger's words caused me to leap out of my skin. It still terrified me how I couldn't sense this guy. That, and him capable of turning into a mass murderer, made me far more jumpy than usual around him.

"Gunther made a fool of himself in front of you. I was just explaining it to everyone else," Milla said.

"No, I didn't." I almost overlapped Milla's speech, like an insecure teenager protecting his fleeting reputation.

Roger still held his side but gave me a warm enough smile I thought was genuine. I really, really hated not being certain. "On the contrary, Gunther, you showed a lot of bravery out there. No need to feel embarrassed."

The words I wanted to say remained behind my lips.

"Have you heard the news? About the Dark Wizard making a bridge to Veniloria?" Tara asked.

The smile dropped from Roger's face. "Yes. I've tried to warn everyone that the Dark Wizard is growing in power. Your tiny group is the only one willing to do what is necessary to get rid of him. Perhaps its numbers shall grow now. I owe it to my wife's memory to make sure these lands are safe for everyone."

I cleared my throat, remembering how much of an insensitive jerk I was about Roger's wife. "An honorable goal, but there is little we plan to do. Except... wait."

This revelation didn't just alarm Roger. "Wait?" Paldric asked.

"Vaywell's position makes it perfect for a strong keep. We can defend the city from the oncoming horde. We just need to fortify it." I almost convinced myself.

"How do you know the Dark Wizard will come here?" Roger asked.

I scrambled to think of something. "He'll be after the artifacts."

"Artifacts?" Roger rubbed the back of his head, his face twisted in thoughts I couldn't read. "I heard from legends one of them was here. Do you think they'd try to steal it?"

Paldric pointed toward the manor house. "Both the sword and shield are here. Lord Adrijian has them." My stomach lurched, and I bit back the desire to tell my main character to shut up. I didn't intend to give Roger *this* much information.

Despite the far too willingly given info, it still didn't convince Roger. "So, the Dark Wizard will risk his entire horde to come here for a pretty sword and shield? I mean, they are artifacts, but without an elf, they're nothing more than any other weapon. Well, no, they'd be some of the best made weapons from the mythical age, but nothing to change the course of a war."

No one said anything. No doubt because of the glare I gave everyone while Roger had his back to me. The message in my look was clear: no one was to reveal Alwin's secret. The reason Paldric didn't blurt it to a semi-stranger was because this was Alwin's secret, and not his to give.

My elf, however, used this opportunity to test the waters. He wouldn't say anything, but he wanted to quiz Roger's intelligence, which would help him understand how weary he needed to be of him.

Roger's frown deepened. He turned to me, which made me drop my glare. He studied my face, no doubt taking in my admittedly plain human features, before studying the others. His eyes settled on Alwin, noticing his exceptional good looks despite the injuries. Noted the grace, strength, and the way he held himself even though humans raised him. Roger turned his head enough to see Alwin's ears, and once he did, my elf knew the man was clever.

Roger bowed. "Master Elf."

Alwin glanced around to make sure no one from the dwindling crowd heard. "I am not here to rule. And I'd rather this secret stay as small as possible. Can you do that?"

"Of course, Master Elf."

"Meaning you just call me Alwin."

Roger bowed again. "Of course, Alwin."

Tara stood up, making sure Paldric was alright before she focused on the group. "So, we're going to stay here in Vaywell? Prepare for a war? With the entire armies of South Island headed straight for us?"

"If that's the plan, we must tell my aunt and uncle at once," Roger said.

My feet were already carrying me toward the manor house when I stumbled at Roger's words. I spun around, staring at him. "What did you just say?"

"Roger has noble blood," Paldric said.

Staring at Paldric helped me realize Roger mentioned this while on their walk. The walk which was soon interrupted by two hundred goblins. I returned my gaze to Roger, trying my hardest to keep my face neutral, but inside I was bellowing in terror. "And, um, your parents?" The words tumbled out of me.

"Right." Roger rubbed the back of his neck. "I don't want anyone to feel bad about me, it happened when I was just a kid, but they're gone. My aunt and uncle have always been like my parents." His words trailed off as I stared at him with horror.

**"Looks like there's another orphan in the group,"** Devin mumbled.

You should have told me!

**"I just learned about his parentage with you."**

No, you should have told me Roger was nobility. That he's a relative to Lady Ana and Lord Adrijian.

**"I thought I had."** He paused, most likely scrolling through our conversations. **"Oh, you're right. I guess**

**I didn't. Sorry, there were other more important things to go over."**

More important? *More* important? No. This is *really* bad.

**"I don't get it."**

Lady Ana and Lord Adrijian are next in line to the throne. And if I'm not mistaken, the Rogue Narrator would've made Roger next. Which means I'm staring at the future King of Veniloria if, I don't know, an entire army of cursed creatures slaughtered his aunt and uncle.

# Chapter Seven

# WE PUT THINGS BACK IN PLACE

Esme was confused when I told her I hated chess. One night, after—

Oh, right. Um, I feel compelled to break up that wonderful opening paragraph to remind everyone that Esme is my ex-wife. With my large readership of exactly five people, I doubted anyone needed that refresher. I certainly didn't. Therefore, this entire "remind the reader because it's a sequel" paragraph is pointless. But let me reiterate because I need the word count: Esme is my ex-wife. Emphasis on 'ex', not so much on 'wife'.

Let's try that again.

Esme was confused when I told her I hated chess. One night, after I returned from Professor Andrews' lecture, I wanted to—

No, I am NOT breaking this up again to remind people about Professor Andrews. Come on, it's not like he's a reoccurring side character. I gave him a fleeting mention in book one about his writing technique lectures, which is all I'm doing now! I would weave the information about him in the paragraph itself, just like he taught me in narration class. Devin, you need to check this device. It's getting a mind of its own.

One night, after I returned from Professor Andrews' lecture, I wanted to discuss it with Esme. He mentioned how crafting a story was like chess. Strategically placing your pieces on the board to keep the other person guessing until you won their hearts. Professor Andrews may have been the top professor at my university, but this was one analogy I disagreed with.

Which is why I talked to Esme about it. After explaining the lecture, she sided with Professor Andrews, which irked me. It also didn't help when she started laughing after realizing how little I actually knew about chess. I don't know about it because I don't play it, and I don't play it because I already knew I wouldn't like it. Being slow and strategic against another player was never a game I enjoyed. Esme tried to explain that there were common moves players did, like popular tropes, to win the reader over.

Except narrating differed completely from chess because I was the only one playing the game. If anything, writing was like that one contraption, the name of which eluded me. Where you set up random stuff and then someone nudges a ball, which magically knocks things over or moves things around. Esme told me the name, but I promptly forgot because she was using her condescending voice. That voice makes me forget whatever she talked about. It's science. Certain levels of condescension triggers an unnatural amount of petty spite in me, which dumps whatever information she's telling me right out of my brain.

Those devices are more the art of crafting a story. They're oh so satisfying. I set things up, and the characters weave seamlessly through the plot points how I want them to. No one bothers me while I work alone.

But this? This was now chess. And I suck at chess almost as badly as titling my books. And I still am kinda not that great at writing women. Or writing refresher information at the beginning of sequels. On the bright side, my rambling must have swelled the word count. I must have gotten at least six or so paragraphs.

Roger stared at me as I finished having my melt down that dissolved into this long, internal monologue. He watched, hiding everything behind that stupid, stoic face of his. I turned around, wanting to return to the manor house. Paldric told Roger where the artifacts were, and I needed to see them personally before I could relax.

A chat with the Lord and Lady of Vaywell was also essential. If they didn't already know, they would now. The entirety of South Island was coming to Vaywell. There were too many things for the cursed creatures to *not* come here. Me, Alwin, the artifacts, and now, if they slaughtered the Lord and Lady who I never bothered giving children (because I didn't *know* there'd be a situation where they were up for the throne), Roger would take over everything.

My steps got longer and faster. My characters fell in behind me.

No, wait. I could no longer say my characters, because not all of them were mine. This made things needlessly complex. It was such an easy defining word, too. My characters. Simple, to the point, painted a clear picture of who was behind me. I didn't have to clutter the sentence with a bunch of proper nouns.

Fine. I can adapt. It can't be that hard. Trying this again.

My characters (and Roger) walked behind me. Tara naturally fell between Roger and Paldric.

"I would love to show you my home here in Vaywell. It has a lovely view of the sea," Roger said.

"That would please me very m—"

"Sounds great," I said to cut Tara off. Roger glanced at me, a slight frown on his face. "The invitation is to everyone, right?"

"It is, yes." Roger's emotions were impossible to read, but I could guess he wasn't happy.

"Wonderful! I look forward to it."

Being of noble birth, I could just imagine the cash Roger had. Especially if he had a home by the sea here in Vaywell. He probably had a sick bachelor pad. Or... or whatever a sick bachelor pad translated to in an epic fantasy setting. It didn't matter. He still had one, and I refused to let Tara go there alone.

We went through the city, passing soldiers with wrapped injuries, while other men went to gather goblin remains to burn. A heaviness hung in the air. We had won this brief battle, but it meant a war would come. Alwin and Paldric talked quietly, as Tara gave Roger a shy smile as they walked in silence.

**"You've clearly decided to stay,"** Devin said.

Right. Devin and the others. I sort of forgot you were there.

**"Understandable. You were busy. Jim left to get other work done. He wanted me to let you know."**

**"I'm still here, though,"** Grace said.

Hello.

**"Alright, Gunther. Let's find common ground. You know how dangerous this is, right?"** Devin asked.

Completely. How many words do I have left?

**"About fifty-six thousand,"** Grace said.

I rubbed my head, trying not to let my characters (and *that* one) notice I was having a silent conversation with other people.

This meant I haven't even reached fifteen thousand words in the new sequel yet. It was a start, but so much happened. We should be at twenty thousand at least.

**"Does this mean you believe the second you hit seventy-thousand words, you're going to end the story? No matter where we are? No matter what your characters are doing?"** Devin asked.

Absolutely. This book will never get published, so it doesn't matter what cliffhanger ending we get. As soon as we hit the word count, I'm out. The story ends, even if it's unfulfilling. My characters will be out of the Rogue Narrator's hands, and that's what I want. Trying to defeat the Dark Wizard is the plot that keeps the device going. My actual goal is to help my characters reach seventy thousand words in one piece.

**"And so, you're going to wait around for war to come to you and *hope* you don't use your powers?"** I sensed the fear trickling through Devin's voice.

If I play my cards right, I won't even need to describe the war. Just the preparations for it. A lot of character building things can happen in fifty-six thousand words while waiting for a war to happen.

**"None of this comforts me at all. You're at fifty-three percent."**

Again, Devin, I know. I'm playing a risky game, but Roger is literally right there. If I leave, he becomes a beacon to all cursed creatures everywhere, and I can't let the Rogue Narrator get my characters.

**"Fine."** Devin didn't sound thrilled. **"It's my duty as Guardian to emphasize how incredibly dangerous this is."**

Lord Adrijian's manor house came into view. Fifty-six thousand more words to describe our preparations. Deepen the bond between Tara and Paldric. It feels like enough. We might not even make it to the war in this book. Then I'll leave and meet all of you in real life. If I remember right, Grace even offered to introduce me to some of her grandchildren.

**"That's right. Say the word, and I'll have Little Nora send you an invitation to her next tea party."**

A smile crossed my face as we walked through the gates. I needed something to anchor me to the real world. Some kind of adventure. Maybe adventure was the wrong word.

I needed something mundane, yet meaningful. And a tea party with a... how old is she?

**"Three years old. Almost four,"** Grace said.

A tea party with a three-year-old was just the thing. Oh. And also checking in on my parents. Are they okay?

**"They are worried sick about you. We update them constantly on your progress. We'd let them come talk to you, but it's way too dangerous. They might say your name,"** Devin said.

My mind froze at the possibility. Gunther, of course, wasn't my real name, because I don't look like a Gunther. I used my powers to forget it pretty early in book one. If I said my name, the story, my characters, possibly even me, would disintegrate and cease to exist, floating around in a pool of other shredded stories. It didn't sound pleasant, and I wanted to keep myself away from that possibility. Even if it meant not talking to my parents the entire time I was in here.

"Gunther?" Alwin asked.

It wasn't until I heard my fake name that I realized I had stopped in my tracks. I glimpsed the limbo world not that long ago, and it was enough to make me shudder.

Tara approached me. "Are you alright?"

"It's fine." I forced my feet to move, crossing the lawn to the manor house. "I'll be fine."

Another thing anchored me to the real world. Get out in fifty-six (possibly now fifty-five) thousand words to check on my parents. To ease their worry. Even though I was a twenty-nine-year-old man, my parents would never stop worrying about me.

**"I give you my word I will not try to convince you to—"** Devin's words were briefly cut off, **"—if you reinstate the code. My word is all I can give."**

My feet carried me into the manor house, heading down the hall as I decided.

You can ease the plot to how you see fit at sixty percent instead of forty-five, and then I will reinstate the code.

**"Gunther—"**

It is my only offer.

Devin's sigh was long, as though using the time to sort through his own pros and cons list. **"Fine. Sixty percent. I'm texting Jim now to have him put together the code."**

Right before the hallway split, I turned to my characters (and the other guy). "Go talk to the Lord and Lady. I will be there in a minute."

They nodded before heading to the throne room. I walked down the other hall, feeling dread. Sequels often had early cliffhangers when characters realized the objects in their possession actually weren't in their possession at all. Like when a character unwraps a sacred object, only to find a broken branch instead. Knowing my luck, a goblin might have snuck in and stolen the artifacts, but maybe not. It was a nice, hot day, and the sunlight drove them nuts. Even in the moonlight, goblins weren't known for stealth missions. The artifacts would still be there. They had to be.

My hand twisted the knob as I opened the door in an extremely calm manner before sauntering in to see the artifacts behind the glass. The three soldiers were, at a glance, my untouched characters. My eyes took in the beautifully carved nymphs on the hilt of the sword and the images of creatures wrapped around the shield before I sighed. No cliffhanger fake artifact this time.

A pressure appeared in my head, and I groaned in surprise. The guards were not concerned about this erratic behavior around priceless artifacts at all and watched me walk out of the room without exchanging glances of concern. Once outside the room, I closed my eyes to sense the new code. The Guardians (Jim, Grace, Devin, and Vince) could ease the plot along once I reached sixty percent. It also erased the restriction of anyone talking about me leaving the story. It gave me a slim eight percent before they could arrange my plot, but it would have to do. Every second I was above fifty percent was not lost on me. Jim was right. No one made it this far, and it wasn't something to celebrate.

"I agree with the code."

**"Good. I'm glad you understand the seriousness of the situation. There will be no book three. Are we clear?"**

I raised my hands ever so slightly. "This series stays a duology."

**"Good."**

"What duology are you reading?" Roger asked.

Did I scream? What is a scream? Can one open their mouth and make noise and it not be a scream? Is it defined when the startled sensation is there? Am I just asking all these questions to avoid saying what happened?

Roger looked embarrassed. "Sorry. I didn't mean to make you scream."

My teeth ground together. "Let's not worry about it."

"I didn't realize you were capable of such a high—"

"What do you need, Roger?" His character, so close to the room with the artifacts, made me sweat.

"My aunt has questions, so I came to find you."

"Right." I didn't like the reminder of Roger's relation to her.

"And I wanted to talk with you." I watched him, once again hating how I couldn't tell what he was thinking.

"You've made it perfectly clear I'm not welcome in the group."

I stopped myself mid-nod to keep my insensitive jerk levels at a healthy minimum. He was right, though. He could sneak up on me, and I was uncomfortable about what he could do with that ability, especially near the room with artifacts.

My silence pushed him to continue. "But understand we are both grown men, capable of putting aside our differences if it means keeping others protected. And I believe we have similar people we'd like to protect."

"Yeah." My eyes narrowed ever so slightly. That was the main issue, though, wasn't it? I didn't know how long Roger wanted to protect them. The longer I studied him, the more I wanted to will myself to read him.

**"Gunther..."** Devin said.

But I didn't. Roger, as far as anyone could tell, was a regular person. This needed to be treated with care. I started walking toward the throne room. "I'm assuming these people you want to protect are Paldric, Alwin, Milla, and Tara?"

"Of course."

"I just needed a verbal confirmation." *Because if needed, I will remind you of this.*

Roger looked confused. "I have always been an honest person, Gunther. I don't know how else to prove it to you except swear I could never harm your friends."

I gave a half smile. "And I want to trust you, Roger. I really do. But you hardly know us."

Roger did not return my smile, but he didn't seem angry. What was that man thinking? "This is how you trust people. You just do it."

We approached the throne room, and I gave Roger one more cautious look. "I'll try."

And I would. The Rogue Narrator backed me into a corner. It was clear my distrust was dangerous, even if it made sense. If I wasn't careful, my characters could turn on me. So I would let Roger be a part of the group. For now.

# Chapter Eight

# TRANSFERRING POWER

Every question Lord Adrijian and Lady Ana had, I answered. Once they realized the severity of the situation, messengers dispersed to every remaining town in Veniloria. South Island had a bridge, and the cursed creatures were on the mainland. After the destruction of Dalehaven, there was solid reason to believe their next target was Vaywell. Messengers left to find any able-bodied men in the surrounding towns who could arrive in less than a day. Then we prepared for a war that I hoped would come to an anticlimactic end of us just... not attending it and everyone arriving in the database instead.

Lord Adrijian began giving orders about what to do to fortify the city, and we went to work. The women and children prepared to leave for safety.

Sometimes I miss the instant communications of cell phones and email. Granted, if we had those, transportation would be quicker, too, and the cursed creatures would already be here.

Which caused a strange image in my mind of goblins riding a truck, some of them sticking their heads out of windows like dogs. Crazy, rabid dogs intent on killing.

What would their road trip music selection be?

A servant placed dinner in front of me, breaking my reverie. Thinking back about the subject of my daydream made me wonder if I was seriously okay.

"Gunther?"

It took a second before I realized Paldric didn't just say my name, but asked a question I didn't hear. I was too busy wondering about a goblin's road trip playlist. I cleared my throat, thankful for the ability to know the question from his face. "Yes, it makes sense for Tara to stay. We need all the healers we can in the coming battle."

Tara didn't look at me, playing with the potatoes on her plate. "I didn't need your permission."

"No, you don't." I picked up my utensils and dove into my dinner. "And Milla should stay, too."

The usual clanking of spoons and forks stilled before all my characters (and stoic man) looked at me. I finished cutting a piece of potato and placed it in my mouth before meeting everyone's gaze. "What?"

"No." My dear elf. Straight to the point, as always. "She should not stay here. Vaywell will turn into a battlefield soon. It's no place for a child."

"And I understand the concern." I would have elaborated, but Roger was sitting next to Alwin.

Tara's eyes narrowed. "You cannot seriously think that's a good idea."

Alright, they needed more information. I would have to be delicate. "She needs to stay near me for... reasons." The ability to describe sensitive things with clarity was not an attribute on my own character list.

But Paldric caught on. Milla needed to stay because she told me my percentage. "Can't you just change her power to someone else?"

Roger glanced at him, frowning. "Her power?"

My gaze settled on the little girl who quietly ate her dinner. She met my gaze, and I understood her thoughts. Despite the obvious dangers of a literal war, she wanted to face it instead of leaving with other women and children. She needed little convincing to stay.

"You've got to think about what's best for Milla," Alwin said.

"I *am* thinking about what's best for Milla. She would be safer in the depths of Vaywell."

Roger tried to return to eating, but set his utensils down again with a clank. "I trust the soldiers to protect Vaywell, but if Milla can leave for safer towns, she should."

"If Tara can make a choice, can't I too?" Milla piped up.

A smile threatened to crack my face, but I kept it hidden as the group turned toward her.

Tara started the onslaught of dialogue. "You're a child."

"It would be safest," Alwin said.

"You've had your own share of hardships," Paldric said.

I sipped my wine, saying nothing. "Gunther wants me to stay." Milla's voice revealed her annoyance and fear.

"He is outvoted," Roger said.

In order to not glare at Roger, I sawed my baked potato in half.

"I don't want to leave. Let me stay with all of you. Please," Milla said.

Paldric shook his head. "It's not safe. I'm sorry, but you've got to leave with the other women and children."

Milla looked at them all before meeting my gaze again. The cogs in her brain began turning, plotting how to hide when the women and children left. That she did this all while staring at me proved this girl had guts. Her thoughts were so easy to read as she formed a simple yet effective plan.

*Stop me if you don't want me to,* she said in her mind, almost a challenge. I said nothing, my eyes softening ever so much as I returned to my dinner. She had her permission, and I was at ease.

"Convince me why an eight-year-old girl should stay during a battle between the forces of good and evil, Gunther, and I will be the first to drop the subject," Roger said.

Everyone turned to face me. I took a drink to keep myself preoccupied. The incredulousness was plain on everyone's face. Even stoic Roger's.

"The Dark Wizard knows about Milla." I looked at no one as I spoke. If the little girl wasn't already planning how she would secretly stay in Vaywell, I'd be freaking out. "If he discovered she wasn't with us, he'd kidnap her to draw us out."

"He'll never know," Roger said.

"On the contrary. He is a Wizard, therefore... quite knowing," I said.

"Does the evil God who created the Dark Wizard know?" Tara mentioning the evil God caused me to wince.

"Evil God? Is this an urban legend in your town?" Roger asked.

The word 'urban' confused my characters, but considering they had to deal with me the past two weeks, they let it slide. But seriously, Rogue Narrator? When you created Roger, you just *had* to keep his modern language? You didn't stop to think that *maybe* "urban legend" would be a weird word in a medieval fantasy story?

Paldric didn't let the silence last long, and he just loved giving information to Roger. "The evil God created the cursed creatures we're about to fight."

Roger's stoic face focusing on something just out of sight. "Yeah, maybe I have heard that somewhere. It feels right. A good God wouldn't create evil creatures."

Silence settled around the table. Paldric was getting way too comfortable with the idea of telling Roger everything, so I kept going to stop him from revealing anything else. "This evil God is omnipotent. All knowing," I added in case my characters (yes, just my characters) didn't understand what omnipotent meant. "He would know if Milla left our group and would try to steal her. What would you do if he succeeded?"

No one said anything, but it didn't matter. I knew what they'd do. Alwin would disappear and no one would find him again until Milla was safe, or he'd die trying. Paldric would rally a troop for a special mission to bring her back, and Tara would volunteer to be part of it. And Roger? I wasn't sure, but when his eyes hardened, I figured it was something to do with protecting her, no matter what. At least, while he wasn't under the Rogue Narrator's code.

"Please don't make me leave." Tears shimmered in her eyes. Oh, she was good, saying all that while forming her master plan.

Paldric cleared his throat. "While I admit it's a possibility, the likelihood of it happening is very low."

"We need to think about what makes you the safest," Roger said.

My main character got out of his chair and walked over to her. He knelt on the ground, holding her arms. "I promise you, once the battle is done, once we take care of the cursed creatures, I will come find you. And we will celebrate with the biggest feast of your life."

"Promise?" Milla asked.

"Promise. You went through too much. Spiders, arrows, a shark, a dragon. It's time you rest." Milla hugged Paldric, and he hugged her back. Roger frowned, then glanced at me, his emotions difficult to figure out.

**"The list of creatures Paldric just rattled off shocked him. He can't help but find fault how you let an eight-year-old be in that situation,"** Devin translated.

My fault? How did he just assume it was my fault when it was Paldric who said it all? Besides, it wasn't... okay, yes; it was partially my fault Milla was there, but it wasn't like I abandoned her to those creatures.

Wait, how do you know all this?

**"I get bits and pieces of his code. Not every time, but enough."**

That's handy. Keep telling me if they pop up.

Roger finished his meal and stood up, looking out the window. "There's more sunlight left in the day. We should use it to our advantage to get that moat dug."

Alwin finished his own plate. I walked toward Milla, Paldric, and Tara. The hug and pep talk from Paldric made the little girl doubt whether to stay, and I needed her to be firmer in her plan.

"I might as well do this now." I made sure Alwin distracted Roger with moat plans before placing a hand on her shoulder. "Things have changed, Milla, and even if you were to stay, I don't want you on the battlefield telling me my percentage."

At first, I wanted to give the power to Paldric, but Tara would be better. She knew how dangerous I could be. While holding Milla's shoulder, I touched Tara's, transferring the ability. With that, Milla realized this was the last thing keeping her among the group. She remembered how good a man Paldric was, who never broke a promise to her. However, her "usefulness" in the group was lessened with this transfer of power. Her plan resumed of how to stay. Perfect.

Tara frowned, receiving the information. "Fifty-three percent. That's dangerously high, Gunther."

"I know."

"And all the cursed creatures are heading straight for us."

I sighed. "I know."

Her eyes studied my face, beginning to form her secret plan of killing me before I reached ninety percent. Her chest rose with a hidden gasp when she noticed the smallest twitch of my eyebrow. The rest of my face remained unreadable, but she still knew I knew.

"Your plan has my support. Don't let me get that high. Please," I said.

She nodded before taking Milla's hand. "Come along, Milla. I'll help you pack. I can even braid your hair if you'd like."

The little girl glanced behind her shoulder, frowning. She still had her plan, and I needed to never think about her hiding spot.

Paldric patted my shoulder. "You're doing the right thing. Milla's safety is vital, therefore she needs to leave Vaywell."

I said nothing, just watched as Milla and Tara headed toward the guest rooms in Lord Adrijian's manor house. The Dark Wizard would do everything in his power to kidnap Milla if she took one step out of Vaywell. Since she already had a plan, the best thing I could do was pretend to agree.

"Roger's right. There isn't a lot of sunlight left." I glanced out the windows. "We should get out and help."

Paldric and I left the manor house. We walked toward the edge of the city, and I saw the people preparing for war. There was a nervous atmosphere in the port city. Most of the men were outside the archway, digging the moat beginning to circle around the town, filling it with spikes. The project was ambitious, but we needed to save Veniloria. Which meant I needed to describe the moat digging and the preparations for battle to the best of my ability to fill this word count. The more I described, the closer I got to the end of the book. This battle couldn't happen. It was too dangerous for me. Being the narrator, I knew Tara wasn't lying. She would try to kill me if I ever reached ninety percent. And I tried really, *really* hard not to realize how little her plan would work if I ever got to that point.

# Chapter Nine

# TEAM PALDRIC

Every so often, I reminded myself it was autumn. It was the next day, and it was hot by the sea. Other places by the sea didn't get hot, but Vaywell did. My glasses slid down my sweaty nose as the rays of the sun continued to warm everything up. I took my shovel and digged into the—

Wait. Digged? No, that doesn't sound right. Dugged? Dug? I think it's dug. I don't have my phone to check.

I took my shovel and dug into the dirt. Paldric and Alwin were on either side of me, doing the same menial task. Roger was nowhere in sight, which was fine unless I thought about it too hard. We were silent, spurred by the need to finish this. The women and children used this day to pack and prepare. Reports were in. As predicted, the cursed creatures were heading straight for us, and would arrive in less than four days. Which gave me three days to describe everything I could and hope the device picked it up. I didn't want to narrate one long battle scene where everyone died. That would be so depressing.

Paldric was quiet and thoughtful. He fell back into a habit of getting the job done. Which meant going about it and not bothering anyone, even though we were all right here. We digged... nope, dug. Dug?... dug into the earth while other men sharpened spikes to dig... yes, dig into the trench, pointed toward the forests. We kept it going all the way around the city. We made good progress, but it was hot.

"Hot day, isn't it?" Roger's cheery voice grated my nerves. I glanced up to see him, like the rest of us, covered in sweat as he held two buckets of water. "Take a break, men. You need to hydrate."

Alwin frowned. "Hydrate?"

"Yeah." Roger said it like everyone had a modern vocabulary in a medieval fantasy. I don't pretend to have a perfect understanding of the history of words, but I definitely wouldn't use a word like hydrate right now. "Drink up. We can't have anyone passing out."

The point of my shovel sank into the ground as I leaned against it, wiping the sweat from my brow. It was still mid-morning. We hadn't reached the hottest part of the day yet. Roger fanned himself with the collar of his shirt as

Alwin took a drink with the ladle. Despite being drenched in sweat like the rest of us, Alwin took the oppressive heat and it somehow looked great on him. And it didn't help that his sweat smelled like fresh flowers.

Elves.

I waited for my turn, remembering in my real life how they hooked me up to an IV in a wing of the hospital and I could never get dehydrated.

"Hot day, isn't it?" Roger asked again, blinking at the sky.

Paldric nodded as he grabbed a ladle full of water. "We're getting a lot done, though. I'm proud of how everyone has come together."

"Indeed." Roger was positively beaming, still fanning himself with his shirt. "It's incredible. Now, I'm not only handing out water but also passing the word along. I've talked to my aunt and uncle, and we want to strengthen the morale of the men." I took the ladle from Paldric and dipped it into the water. "We're going to have a ball tonight before the women and children leave."

The ladle slipped on the way to my mouth and dropped toward the dirt. I did that thing where I tried to catch it, but part way there, realized it was pointless and shoved my hand in my hair, instead. The ladle clattered to the ground. "Sorry, a what?"

"A ball. Dance. Party. Send off our women the right way. Give these men some happy memories with their women to remind us why we need to fight to protect them," Roger said.

My eyes were wide as I stared at him, the horror plain on my face. Alwin picked up the ladle, brushing the dirt off. I didn't narrate dances. I hardly wrote parties. My genre was... I wrote epic fantasy adventures. I didn't know the first *thing* about dancing. Fine, yes, book two was going to be about parties and feasts, but that was back when I was supposed to get out. People with actual skill at writing dances and parties were supposed to write it. Not *me*. Especially not if the Rogue Narrator suggested the idea in the first place.

A smile crossed the face of my quiet, thoughtful main character. "That sounds like a wonderful idea."

And Paldric and Tara... and Roger... all at a dance...

"It is such a hot day! I hope you men will excuse me," Roger said.

And then the stoic man just took off his shirt. My jaw dropped, even as I tried not to let it. I stared at his ridiculously ripped torso with contempt. Roger smiled at Alwin before grabbing the ladle and pouring some water on top of his head. I glared. Tara could never see this man shirtless.

How did he even get this ripped? I realized, now, why romance writers described doing laundry on abs, because this man probably did. Wait, two, four, six... was that *eight*! How did this guy get an *eight pack*? How could he... did he have an entire gym in his bachelor pad here in Vaywell?

"Seriously?" was all I could sputter.

Roger looked confused. "Oh, I'm sorry. Did you get a drink yet, Gunther?" He offered me the ladle partially full of water.

My speech tripped on the way out, and I said nothing intelligent. The ball angered me because it was such a good idea, and I would hate every minute. Now the Rogue Narrator was literally showing me what Roger could offer Tara.

I snatched the ladle out of his hands, which caused more water to spill out. I got a dry swallow before throwing it back at him. Roger caught it, still confused, as I grabbed Paldric's arm and pulled him away from the other two.

"Um, Gunther? Are you alright?" Paldric asked.

"Fine. Everything is fine. We're going to weather this storm just fine." We walked past the men digging. Dugging? Nope, it's definitely digging. I hate that word. I hate it so much.

"We both know you're lying. You're being unnaturally obsessed with Roger." Paldric paused, contemplating what he just said. "You notice that too, right?"

"I am exhibiting the perfect amount of attention! If you knew what I knew, you would also exhibit the perfect amount—"

"Gunther," Paldric said again as I yanked him further... farther?... ugh! We got away from Roger. "I just think if you—"

"This is not the time! We have too much to do!"

Paldric sighed but continued to let himself be drugged away... Drugged? No, that has to do with chemicals. Dragged? Why can't I figure out words today? I'm a narrator, for crying out loud!

"Listen, Paldric," I said once Roger and Alwin were far enough away not even my elf could overhear. "That is your competition." I pointed to Roger, who was still shirtless and pouring another ladle of water over himself. "That's who you need to fight off at the ball. You *cannot* let Tara dance with him, alright?"

Paldric frowned. "Gunther, I think you've—"

"Tara likes him. She might even fall in love with him. That cannot happen. Got it? Bring your game. Woo the woman you love. You two have a future together. Babies. Picket fences. At least the equivalent of picket fences in a medieval fantasy. Look at Roger. He's just all brooding bad boy and traumatic past." Paldric glanced at Roger who was, admittedly, laughing at a joke Alwin told, but the traumatic past was true. "You may not think that's a lot, but women eat that up. It doesn't help that he's got a mountain of cash. Tara will want to fix him, to mother him, and she *cannot* develop deeper feelings for him. It's got to be you. You are the nice guy. But, you know, not the nice guy with the strange TM symbol at the top. I don't know what that stands for, but you're not *that* kind of nice guy. You're a genuinely good person, which means you need to fight harder for her affections without turning into a jerk. Remind that woman you are a nice guy without turning into *the* nice guy." I wiggled my fingers in the air. "You know. Nice Guy TM symbol thingy. You can do it."

"Gun—"

"You've got to understand, when women are in a love triangle, they *never* choose the safe option. Because the truth is universal, and everyone acknowledges it: single brooding bad boys with mountains of cash are always on the hunt for women. But that won't happen in this story. Team Paldric all the way." I raised my hand for him to give me a high five.

Paldric blinked at me. Then he blinked again. I grabbed his wrist and forced him to give me a high five. It didn't work well, but it happened. Paldric cleared his throat as he dropped his hand. "Gunther, are... are you *certain* you should stay here? Now that you could leave?"

"I'm fine, Paldric. One hundred percent fine. Okay, well, maybe not a hundred percent. People who say they're a hundred percent fine always lie to themselves, and I do not lie to myself. So, ninety! I am ninety percent fine! Which means I'm perfectly fine!"

This conversation was worrying Paldric, even though he did a pretty good job keeping his cool. "I don't know what you're talking about."

"You are not taking this seriously. Roger could very well swoop Tara off her feet tonight, and I need you to... not. Not let that happen."

My main character glanced again at Roger, finally noticing his ripped muscles and unbelievable eight pack. Paldric became aware his own torso didn't look like that. He ran a hand down his shirt, glancing at me, embarrassed I caught his moment of insecurity, before staring at the ground. "Gunther, I understand this ball might worry you." I snorted, because worried was just one of the words I'd use in this situation if words made sense to me today. "But the way you talk about Tara makes me think you don't actually know her."

I had nothing to say to that. I folded my arms, knowing there were things about Roger that Paldric didn't know either, but my main character needed to have a turn talking. "You act as though Tara will take one look at Roger shirtless and fall in love with him. Honestly, that's as obnoxious as saying a man can't control himself around a scantily clad woman." His words brought a sting of chastisement, because I remembered exactly what happened between me and Tara back in book one. Which proved I was the obnoxious man who couldn't control my thoughts. "Tara's not that kind of person. And if..." A tiny sigh escaped him. "And if it turns out she loves him, then I will step aside. I have always wanted what's best for her, what makes her happy. If Roger makes her happy, why would I stand in the way of that?"

My lips pressed together in a line to keep my groan inside. I grabbed a few locks of my hair, trying not to pull too hard. "You are such a nice guy. No TM sign at all. Oh, this is bad."

Paldric gave me another look. "Come on, Gunther. I think you're putting too much on this ball. It's a fun idea Roger thought of to help the morale of everyone involved. A relaxing evening. We need one of those right now." Of course Paldric would think that, because he didn't realize he was in a story. That we narrators meticulously plan every single scene in order to get the most character development and action to drive the plot forward. My groan came out as a hiss, getting louder the further... farther...

"I HATE WORDS! ALL OF THEM!"

"Gunther?" Paldric was not hiding his worry.

"I'm fine! I need to... get a drink. Of water. In the city." I dropped my hands and headed toward Lord Adrijian's manor house.

"Alright. I will see you later," Paldric said.

My hands were stuffed in my pockets as I stomped away. I glared at the ground before glancing behind my shoulder to see Roger at least had his shirt back on. Paldric returned, patting Roger on the shoulder as they talked a bit more about the upcoming ball. Paldric admitted he didn't know how to dance, and Roger offered to show him some moves, because *of course* the man knew how to dance.

This is going to suck!

# Chapter Ten

## TEAM TARA

The city moved past me as I stormed by, stewing and mumbling to myself.

**"Gunther, you are giving into your need to control, and your percentage is too high for that,"** Devin said.

I shot my glare at the sky before focusing on the road again. True, Roger didn't make a move on Tara, but this was still a chess game that pushed me out of my comfort zone. Maybe this didn't shock anyone, but dances intimidated me. I didn't *want* to do any of this.

Wait, I never said Devin's name to alert him to the device. How are you talking to me?

**"As soon as a narrator hits fifty percent, they're under constant supervision. You don't need to say my name to bring one of us here."**

Right. I was over fifty percent. Sometimes I forgot.

**"Keep forgetting that."**

I walked through the manor house, trying to find Tara.

"Oh, hello Gunther. Returning from the moat so soon," Lady Ana said.

"Just for a moment. I'll get back to dig... digging it, but I need to find Tara."

Lady Ana frowned, thinking about where she saw her last. "I believe she's with Milla in her room, packing."

"Thank you."

"Did you hear about the ball tonight? Are you excited?" Lady Ana asked.

"Absolutely. Can't wait." My voice had no inflection as I headed down the hallway.

Doors passed as I contained my terror.

**"We won't leave you alone. You have my word."**

Because you have to follow the law and not leave me alone.

**"Even if you were at forty-nine percent, one of us would help you out at this ball. Yes, this is a ploy of the Rogue Narrator, so we must treat this carefully."**

My thoughts tried way too hard to seem in control as I came to a partially opened door with familiar voices behind it.

"Milla? Tara?" I knocked.

There was a pause, then the door opened, and Tara stood there, giving me the commonplace distrusting look whenever I was around. "What are you doing here? Shouldn't you be outside the city digging a moat?"

"I was. And I will return, but... but I wanted to check on you."

Tara cocked her head to one side. "Me? Why? What's going on?"

"You heard the news?"

Her face dropped. "Is Paldric alright? Alwin? Roger? Did someone get hurt?" She straightened, ready to follow me to the injured person, but I held out a hand.

"No, no, no. Everyone's fine. I was more asking about the ball."

The worry drained from her face before morphing into a soft glare. It helped me realize how much she didn't enjoy the terror I put her through just then. "You think this ball is an urgent enough matter that you stopped working on protecting the city to make sure I knew about it?"

She was justified in her annoyance, but I didn't want to admit it. But also knew I needed to. So, I just stood there and stretched out every syllable to say, "Yyyeeesss." Tara gave me a darker glare before almost shutting the door, but I placed my palm flat against it to keep it open. "Tara, I need to talk to you. Yes, I'm worried about this ball, and I'd feel better if you understood why I'm so nervous about it."

The sigh she kept back finally released before she opened the door wider. "Alright. I'm listening." She said it so I would give my spiel and leave.

"Look, I know there's a lot about me you don't trust." Her head tilted, and she raised both eyebrows. A face which hinted she believed I just said an understatement. "But I cannot let you attend this ball without me saying you can't... you definitely cannot..." Tara watched me get my foot ready to stuff into my mouth. "I don't trust Roger. I know he may seem nice, and he'll say all the right words, but..."

The way Tara looked at me, clearly humoring me, made me want her to understand how dangerous this was. Maybe I could play this ultra safe.

"I don't think you need either of them. Roger *or* Paldric. You're a strong, independent woman who doesn't need a man to define her. Look at you. You're incredible all by yourself. You should... should take some time. For yourself. To really discover who you are. Go on a journey." I cleared my throat. "Just... don't... actually leave. And don't make any decisions tonight. We'll... get as much description as we can, and... and you won't need to worry about it. Take the time to find yourself. Don't kiss anyone tonight. Unless you are kissing yourself... metaphorically." Tara's face was impossible to read, but I knew she was watching me chomp on my foot, placed so securely in my mouth. She hoped my shoe would dissolve, so I'd actually bite it and be in pain. "Because... because... you know..." I raised my hand to get a high five. "Team Tara."

It did not impress her. She closed her eyes, trying to figure out if she should grab Milla and run or keep glaring at me, so I understood how much of an idiot I was. She opened her eyes, the glare clearly winning the argument as she forced me to lower my hand. "Has anyone told you that you are unnaturally obsessed with that man?"

"It's..." I scratched the side of my jaw, wishing I could give her the information so she understood. Or force her to be terrified.

**"Nope, don't do that."**

My arms folded, aware Devin was right. "He's not a creation of mine. Like you. Or Milla. Or Paldric and Alwin."

"Roger isn't dangerous. He's kind. Sweet, even. He went through a tragedy no one should experience. But I've sensed nothing dangerous from him," Tara said.

My teeth pierced my tongue to keep from growling at Tara's review of Mr. Eight Pack. Once the feeling passed, I cleared my throat again, straightening my glasses. "He probably seems like a regular guy, but I've had the Gods look into him. He has an unpredictable part of him, and no, you may not try to fix it. We don't know what it is, and considering an evil God created him, we can't trust him."

Tara leaned against the door, narrowing her eyes. "So, you're saying because he has a small part of him that might turn on us, we should throw him out?"

"Just don't trust him. That's what you do. Don't get emotionally involved with him, because he will definitely break your heart," I said.

"Because I'm a weak-willed woman who could never function with a broken heart," Tara said, the sarcasm clear.

"He's just dangerous." I kept it short, aware of the perilous territory I stumbled on. It made it worse that I only had one foot since the other was stuffed way down my throat.

"Are you suggesting we hold him at arm's length so he knows how much we distrust him? While also accidentally causing his spiral into that thing that will make him betray us in the end?"

"Yeah, well…" I thought about it. "Yeah, that should work. Roger's a strong enough man he might not spiral." And the book might end before that.

Tara shook her head. "You realize I'm talking about you in a veiled way, right?"

I frowned. "What?"

"*You're* the one that could kill us, and yet we've been happy to let you stay. You've done far worse than Roger ever has, and yet it's *him* you want us to distrust? After the things you've done to us, to *me*, we still welcome you as a member of our group. Now that you know how we treat you, are you seriously demanding I should somehow treat Roger worse? When he's done nothing that comes close to the crimes you've done?"

There was an uncomfortable sting in my soul as I realized how truthful her words were. Above me, Devin chuckled. **"Grace is right. Tara's awesome."**

"It's..." I looked up, gnawing on my proverbial foot. "When you said..." My frown deepened. "I hadn't thought of it that way before." Each word from that sentence was carefully extracted from my soul, as though admitting it would lessen the sting.

Tara gave me a final glare before slamming the door in my face. I waited before resting my head against it and groaned. She was right, of course. I wanted them to treat Roger worse than how they treated me, even though he gave no reason for it.

Dread still percolated through me as I walked away from the hall. This ball would happen, and I was unprepared.

No, not unprepared. Just acknowledging I couldn't do this.

My hand reached out, finding the wall as I leaned down, covering my eyes. "Graaaaaace? I need you. And your experience. As a woman. Have you written about dances?"

**"I'll patch her in. Give me a moment,"** Devin said.

I rubbed my forehead, feeling sick. What was it about dances that made me nauseous? Much like a romantic subplot, I didn't understand why it worked for other people, and yet never worked for me. And now I was being thrown into a ball where the Rogue Narrator knew what he was doing.

**"Hello, Gunther dear. You need my help?"** Grace asked.

My back straightened as I headed out of the manor house. "Yes. We're having a ball tonight."

**"Ooh! Yay, I love balls!"** She clapped. **"Masquerade?"**

"Um, normal? I think normal ball? If that's a thing?" My face crumpled at the thought of a masquerade. I did *not* want one of those. "I don't know what I'm doing. Even with a regular dance."

**"Oh, well, I've never written balls myself. I'm the poetry writer of the group, but don't you worry. We'll get Jim on here too. He's written quite a few dances."**

**"He has?"** Devin asked.

"**Of course! Didn't you ever read his Night Force? I swear my daughter's reading glasses fogged up from how steamy that scene was.**"

*Jim* knew how to write balls? I closed my eyes, running my hands down my face. It didn't matter. As long as *someone* who had my back knew what they were doing.

"**Between Jim and I, we will take care of you. Oh, I'm so excited!**" Grace said.

I did not feel the same.

# Chapter Eleven

# Team Roger If Paldric Wasn't Clearly the Better Option

A great way to work stress out was to drive a sharp metal object into the ground repeatedly. It helped with stress a little, though despite the gloves I wore, blisters formed on my hands. I didn't realize how badly they hurt until the day was done and I eased the gloves off.

My elf approached me, looking at my hands. "First time digging a moat?"

"The heavens don't need moats." I curled my fingers. "Isn't this the first time for you, too?"

Alwin glanced down at his hands that were, of course, perfect. Not a callous or blister, like he hadn't spent all day digging. "I've done some work with my hands before."

"Yeah, you're right. You've digged some holes. Dug. You've... dug... holes." Alwin gave me a confused look. "I don't have my phone to check what word is correct."

Alwin's confusion did not lessen.

**"It's dug,"** Devin said.

My hand patted his shoulder, which I instantly regretted. "Let's get you cleaned up. I'm sure you'll be busy dancing all night."

"Why?"

"No reason." We walked into the city. My dear elf wouldn't realize how good looking he was, which meant women would surround him all night.

I cleaned up as best I could. Lord Adrijian let me borrow one of his more formal set of clothes. I brought it back to my room when Devin logged off, wishing me a good night. A long night's sleep was too tempting for him not to take. Grace was there, but she turned off her second screen so I could get dressed. I appreciated it, even though it was dangerous to do to someone over fifty percent.

**"Oh, I trust you,"** Grace said.

Is Jim on yet?

**"Not yet. He should be here shortly, though."**

My thoughts jumbled as I tried to think of something to say. I hoped having a conversation with Grace would help me forget there was a ball about to happen, and I would be responsible for the safety of my characters.

**"It'll be alright Gunther, dear. You prepared your characters well."**

Did I? My original outline didn't have a ball planned, and now the Rogue Narrator wanted to have one. I can't help but feel terrified.

**"Hello Gunther, this is Jim, logging on."**

Hi, Jim.

**"What a sharp-looking suit you've got on."**

"Thanks." I grabbed the coat portion and put it on, feeling how big it was in the shoulders.

**"Does this mean I can turn on my second screen?"** Grace asked.

"Yeah, go ahead." I tried to resist the desire to squeeze the extra cloth together. Lord Adrijian was also broad shouldered. Like uncle, like nephew.

**"You look very handsome, dear,"** Grace said.

My nod was lame. Technically, this night wasn't about me. It was keeping Roger away from Tara as much as possible.

**"Oh, we could do more than that! We'll deepen Paldric and Tara's relationship too!"** Grace said.

Despite the joy in Grace's voice, her words filled me with dread. Yeah, I got to work on them, too.

**"I've been thinking a lot about your situation, Gunther, and I have a letter here I'd like to read to you,"** Jim said.

"Oh, is it long?" Maybe Jim was about to add a lot more words to the total count.

He chuckled. **"No. Not too terribly long. It's from your parents."**

Without meaning to, I flinched. My thoughts occasionally drifted to my parents, but it was almost easier to assume I was on a long trip and couldn't get a hold of them. Most of the time, I just convinced myself they were fine. Truth was, they were probably freaking out. I pushed thoughts of them away in order to cope with my situation. Knowing Jim had a letter from them to give me a glimpse into their thoughts made me sink into the side of the bed.

**"Would you like me to read it?"** Jim asked.

My fingers tangled through my hair. I didn't fix it for this ball, so it didn't matter if I messed it up more. "Go ahead. I'd... like to hear from them."

**"Dear Son,"** Jim began. **"We think about you every day. Please know we love and care about you and hope for the day you can live in our basement again."**

I couldn't help but snort, then looked at my shoes so Grace and Jim didn't notice the tears forming in my eyes.

**"You may not think that's the best living situation right now, but we don't care. We are eager to welcome you back, because you'll finally be here again. We were there in the hospital that first week you entered your story, waiting for you to wake up, but we'll continue to wait from home. Dad can't stay away from work for too long. The Guardians give us plenty of updates about your condition and what you've been up to in your story, but we want you to know we don't care what you've done. We want you back. Please. Love, Mom and Dad."**

My arms folded, and I sniffed again before glancing out a window. The Guardians must do this a lot, getting letters from parents or loved ones to convince them to get them out of their story.

**"We do, yes. Your parents are kind people."**

They are. I was lucky to grow up as I did. Lucky to have parents to fall back on when times got tough.

**"They're deeply worried about you, dear."**

A lot of my characters are orphans right now. I hope my parents didn't take it personally.

It was a stupid goal, but maybe I could remember gener-ous parents who offer their basement. Something to look forward to after the book was finished. But I had to attend this ball first.

**"You're over twenty-two thousand words at this point. If we play this right, we can get past thirty-thousand total words tonight, and you'll still have a few more days before the Dark Wizard arrives,"** Jim said.

I rolled my head around my neck. "More description of the ball, so I don't have to end up describing the battle. Less than fifty thousand words left. I can do this. I can do this. Oh, I repeated myself, but that's fine. Pages upon pages of description. I can do this. I said that phrase again, but it works. It's more words. Remember the five senses. Smell, taste, feel, hear, see. Smell, taste, feel, hear, see. I can do this."

As I walked out of my room, the smell of roasted meats hung heavy in the—

Roger grabbed my dinner jacket, shoving me against the wall. I barely had time to cough before he pressed a dagger between my ribs, my glasses sliding down my nose. Despite the incredible danger I was in, I felt amazed Roger already showed his true colors this early into the evening.

"Whoa, Roger. What's going on?" I tried to play it cool, but my voice was higher than it should be.

"Just shut up and listen to me. I've got to get something off my chest, so we're going to do this, face to face," Roger said.

"Face to face? We can't now, since I'm a few inches taller than you are." At this point, I was just blabbering.

"Would you *shut up*!" Roger hissed.

My hands braced against the wall, my flared nostrils the only thing keeping my glasses on my nose.

**"The code isn't there. The Rogue Narrator isn't influencing this action,"** Grace said.

Glad we've established that him threatening me with a dagger is a natural part of his character. I feel so much better now.

"Paldric just told me this absolutely crazy story," Roger said. Placing the tip of a dagger against my ribs probably meant he didn't want me to speak, so I obliged. "He said you tried to rape Tara."

I closed my eyes, feeling... well, I wasn't sure how to describe this feeling. The story was true, and there was no point in denying it. I treated Tara horribly, and deserved to have my life threatened for it, but why did Paldric tell that story to Roger? My main character trusted people way too much and apparently told everyone's life stories.

Unless the Rogue Narrator forced Roger to manipulate the information out of him.

**"Not possible. If it was a direct link from the Rogue Narrator, we would have gotten an alert,"** Jim said.

"So, tell me why I shouldn't ram this dagger straight through your ribs, rapist?"

**"Careful how you go about this, Gunther,"** Jim said.

My hand inched forward to push my glasses back on the bridge of my nose. "Because if you ram a dagger through me, my invulnerability will kick in, and I won't die. If you keep reminding me I'm immortal, I will realize exactly how much power I have. I will force you to be my servant and do my bidding. Or I'll just kill you off because I deem you too untrustworthy."

**"That was... an interesting choice,"** Jim mumbled.

Roger narrowed his eyes, keeping the dagger close. "That is the most ridiculous thing I've ever heard."

"You can test it. Or just remember when you saved me on the battlefield. Cutting through all those goblins before finding me on the dirt, not a speck of my blood showing."

He tightened his grip on the handle of the dagger.

**"Oh, dear. You've made him curious,"** Grace said.

He poked my ribs with the dagger, which honestly tickled. I snorted before pushing his hand away, figuring that was a good enough lesson. "I am fully aware what I did was wrong. And I don't deserve any of the kindness these people have given me. My existence puts everyone in danger."

"You're right." Roger took a step back and gestured at me with his dagger, keeping a hold of my fancy jacket. "They are too kind to you. Which is why I'll spend the rest of my life learning to kill you, in case you have any of these inclinations again."

My hand rubbed my ribs. It didn't hurt, but it couldn't be good for my percentage. Which...

"Gunther?" We both turned to see Tara walking down the hall. "Why do I feel I need to tell you your percentage is—" She stopped at the scene before her. Roger still pinned me against the wall with one hand and held a dagger in the other. "Roger?" The smallest part of her believed this man could be as dangerous as I warned her about, and I considered that a win in this game of chess.

"Paldric told me what Gunther did to you." Roger let go of me and sheathed his dagger. "I wanted to let him know how I felt about his actions."

Just like that, the cautious part of her disappeared, which made me frown. It really should raise more red flags. She moved forward, her heels clicking on the stone floor. "Paldric did mention he told you."

I frowned, studying her face more. It seemed to have been an accidental slip up. Paldric was so used to Roger being part of the group that he spoke about Tara as though the man already knew what happened. Roger, who wasn't there, asked for more clarification in an alarmed manner. My main character hastily gave the bare bones of the story and, for once, seemed abashed that he had told Roger something, later apologizing to Tara.

Tara moved closer to Roger. "I appreciate you not taking this lightly, but Gunther is well aware how vile his actions were, and we don't want to make him realize he…"

His arms folded, eyes narrow. "Why do you keep him around if he might do it again?"

"He wouldn't…" Tara started to say, but stopped. Honestly, she didn't know, and this uncertainty made her realize Roger was right. Why did they keep me around?

Nope, not in this chess game. I had to say something so she wouldn't carry on with that train of thought. "I won't do it again." And I was sure I wouldn't. Even if my percentage hit one hundred, I would still never touch Tara. True, I might kill her with a thought instead, but I wouldn't try to assault her again.

**"Let's not talk about you possibly reaching a hundred percent. Let's keep saying it'll never happen,"** Jim said.

Fair enough.

Tara hesitated, then looked at me. "Have you even told him who you are yet?"

Roger turned his gaze back toward me, and I stared at his unreadable face. "At the rate this is going, I just assumed Paldric would," I said.

Tara's heels clicked closer to us. "He's a God pulled from the heavens, trying to find his way back."

Alright, I guess Tara would start spilling my secrets now. Seems like neither Paldric nor Tara can keep secrets from each other. Basis of a strong marriage right there. They'd never fall into the miscommunication trope. I've trained them so well.

Roger blinked a few times, taking this all in.

**"Taking it super well, actually. It makes sense to him, just like it makes sense to your other characters,"** Jim said.

"So... not the evil God?" Roger asked.

"No." I couldn't look at him. "Just an imperfect one. Fighting my battle with the evil God, as he's trying to destroy everything I created."

Somehow, the weight of the situation brought out the absolute stoicism in him.

**"We're not getting anything either, dear."**

It was a lot to process, considering he did just threaten me. Even now, his fingers brushed against the hilt of the dagger before he sheathed it and folded his arms. "You're a God?"

"And you being here is the reason he won't return," Tara said.

I winced, wishing Tara hadn't brought that up. It was difficult enough to figure out what he was thinking. Roger shot a glance at Tara, frowning. "Me? Why me?" Neither one of us spoke. Tara, despite metaphorically leading Roger to the secret hiding under the blanket, stood aside so I would be the one to reveal it. I didn't want to. Roger's stoicism was intimidating as he faced me. "Why me, Gunther?"

"Because I never created you. The evil God did, and I can't leave without knowing my creations will be alright."

The silence between the three of us stretched on as Roger stared me down, everything in his face hidden from my understanding.

Please tell me someone knows what he's thinking.

**"Nope. Sorry, Gunther,"** Jim said.

The man finally blinked. "The evil God? But—I'm no different from anyone else. I am, and always have been, a citizen of Veniloria."

"Roger," Tara said.

Emotion finally broke through his face, and I recognized the anger. "You're saying I'm created by the same being who made those cursed creatures?" My silence did not help his anger. "You can't prove it. I won't believe it."

The only words I could think of tumbled out of my mouth. "I'm... sorry."

"No!" The stoicism dropped, and anger filled his eyes. "No, I'm not created by the evil God. I'm nothing like the cursed creatures. They slaughtered my wife! We are nothing alike!"

For the first time, I understood him. He was a normal character, with a complex life before he found our group. There was no desire to hurt, not even to hate. And yet part of his code was susceptible to the Rogue Narrator's wishes, and for that reason alone, I couldn't assure him he wouldn't act like a goblin.

"I am not one of them!" Roger moved past Tara. "I will *never* be one of them!"

We watched him leave, both of us unsure what to do. Feelings of compassion for his situation hit, and I would be the first to admit I was wrong about him.

Tara watched him go before turning her attention back to me. "You were almost fifty-four, but you went back to fifty-three. I'm going to finish getting dressed."

Which is when I finally noticed she was wearing a kind of bathrobe thing. She didn't want me to notice because of what happened between us. She clutched the two ends of her bathrobe near her throat as she turned and left. I leaned against the wall, running through the conversation again. Paldric told Roger. Roger threatened to kill me. Tara stopped him. He knows I'm God, and that I didn't create him.

I didn't even begin describing the smells coming from the kitchen.

**"Are you okay, Gunther?"** Jim asked.

Yeah. I think I am.

**"Good. Grace and I will watch Roger through the code. He's gone to an empty guest room now."**

The empty hallway picked up the noises from outside. I didn't know what would happen to Roger, but I trusted Grace and Jim. It was time to attend a ball.

# Chapter Twelve

## I Attend a Ball

The smell of roast meats hung heavy in the air. Which was impressive, considering the banquet was outside. All the citizens of Vaywell couldn't fit in the manor house, so the servants set the tables outside, and everyone brought something to share.

My eyes scanned over the pies, the roasted meats, the entire roasted pig, the salads, the dressings, the punch. I took in the aesthetically pleasing placement of all this food. Different colored fruits, the dark, burgundy roasted meats, the freshness of the salads, of the fruits and vegetables. The people of Vaywell knew how to throw a party, but my cynicism crept in again. The Rogue Narrator proved back in book one that he could control my filler characters. It wouldn't be hard for one of them to bring a poisoned dish, but as I ran my eyes over the food again, I sensed no poison. After putting that initial fear to rest, I closed my eyes and took a deep breath. The food smelled... cozy? The perfectly spiced pork, the pies, the apple, pumpkin, blackberry, blueberry, so many sweet smells mingled with the hearty roasted pig. It somehow worked. And 'cozy' was the word I thought of.

A warm breeze came in through the ocean, the salty air driving my appetite. Laughter sprinkled throughout the gathering, and for this small moment, everyone forgot why the nobility suggested this ball.

**"Gunther, you're missing it,"** Grace said.

Panic surged, and I glanced around. What? What was I missing?

**"Classic. Look at Paldric,"** Jim said.

Neither sounded panicky, but I couldn't help but whirl around, searching the crowd for my main character. He turned out to be not that far from me, and he looked distracted, not even noticing the people around him. It was an incredibly dangerous move. Didn't he realize this was the Rogue Narrator's idea?

**"Oh hush, Gunther. You're completely misinterpreting it,"** Grace said.

What do you mean I was misinterpreting it? He's got to be aware of his surroundings! There were a lot of filler characters here and the Rogue Narrator could—

I followed Paldric's line of sight, which is when I noticed Tara had walked outside, holding Milla's hand. She laughed, moving her arm to help Milla twirl in her dress.

Oh.

**"Look at the guy. Completely enamored."** Jim was right. Paldric had completely forgotten where he was, his eyes only for Tara.

**"Gunther, dear, this is a ball. Describe Tara's dress."**

The small smile I realized had crept up on me instantly faltered. I guess describing her dress would pad the word count.

**"No dress descriptions, you don't have a ball."**

**"Grace is right. No dress descriptions, anarchy will ensue,"** Jim said.

My eyes traveled over her dress in a critical and professional manner. The inner voice of Esme came back, warning me to never mention curves, boobs, or to sexualize the dress in any manner.

The dress was white. And—and it had—had a dark blue ribbon thingy around the bottom of the dress that looked like...yep. Birds.

I winced, then glanced away.

**"Is now a good time to mention your ex-wife was controlling?"** Jim asked.

**"Abusive, really. You were right to end that, dear."**

"She does not speak for the entirety of women everywhere."

Despite my knee jerk reaction to agree with them, it wasn't the only reason I struggled with this. Not too long ago, Grace needed to talk me down from assaulting Tara further. I fell back to simply not mentioning Tara's looks, for fear Esme was right. That I was a shallow, misogynistic pig.

**"Jim, do you want to take this one?"** Grace asked.

**"Sure thing. Just give me a second."** I glanced up at the sky, confused, until Jim started talking again. **"The dress was made with a beautiful white silk and boasted of a full skirt. Embroidered dark blue birds weaved their own sort of dance around the bottom of her dress. It must have been one of Lady Ana's ceremonial dresses. Since Lady Ana was a full head taller, Tara wore blue heels to keep the delicate hem off the ground. Tara was unfamiliar in such a beautiful dress, terrified to touch the silk for fear she would spoil it, and nervous to walk too quickly on the uneven ground. But Paldric knew none of her thoughts, for she captivated him. A quiet thought confirmed she would always be more beautiful than he dared imagine. He admired her dress, saw the dying sunlight reflect off the silk, giving it a golden glow that**

**paled to her glowing face when she looked up and met Paldric's gaze. She smiled back, playing with the sapphire pendant around her neck."**

The interaction played out, tempting me to give Jim full narration rights while in the ball. I'm not sure I could, but he did that interaction justice.

**"Anything to add, Grace?"** Jim asked.

**"She dropped the pendant, and it nestled back onto her cleavage, the kind that makes an old woman reflect of times past when her own breasts were so firm and perky. Oh, to be young again."**

Jim laughed, and I coughed to cover up my own, before feeling bad about it.

**"It won't get published, dear. I can even describe that since she's wearing white, she's clearly not on her period, but I don't see in the code that you scheduled in that bodily function."**

No, I didn't. Not because I'm misogynistic or anything. It's as I mentioned before. I'm bad at math.

**"It's wild the things you can get away with in a story,"** Jim said.

Book logic is not logical.

Tara walked toward Paldric, smiling. "Hello."

"Hello." It was a miracle Paldric got that out, breathless as he felt. "You look beautiful."

"Thank you. You're quite handsome yourself."

Paldric wiggled his toes in his shoes. "It's a miracle what a good washing can do." Tara giggled at his response.

**"Self-deprecating humor when faced with a compliment. Wonder where he gets that from,"** Jim said.

Don't know, but whoever it is must be unnaturally secure in himself.

Jim chuckled as Tara kept a hold of Milla's hand. "Is Lord Adrijian here yet? The food smells incredible."

The sweetness of the pies with the roasted pork was tantalizing. Milla walked over to me, and inspired by Jim's descriptions, I tried a bit of my own.

Milla's dress was a golden color, made of a far sturdier material than silk, but it didn't make it any less beautiful. She had a red strip of... a thing of...

My fingers brushed the inside of my pocket for my phone to look up what that thing was called tied around her waist.

**"Ribbon? Belt? Sash?"** Jim prompted.

I thought sashes were over the shoulder.

**"I'm sure it's a sash,"** Grace said.

It was a red sash around her waist, tied with an enormous bow behind her. She even had golden gloves on her hands. As she got closer, I saw cats embroidered onto her dress, playing with red thread, also embroidered with the red thread. The strangeness of it messed with my head. She ran up to me, giving the dress a half twirl. "Do you like it?"

"Fit for a princess." She beamed at me, and the excitement of the evening almost made her stop plotting how to stay in Vaywell.

"They didn't have nice enough shoes my size, so I'm going barefoot," Milla lifted her skirt enough to show me she was indeed barefoot. She didn't mind. Watching Tara take a few practice steps in her heels while in their room, she opted for the safest option.

Lord Adrijian approached. "My dear citizens of Vaywell, welcome to our ball! We have worked hard, and it is time to party! Centuries from now, they will remember the sacrifices we have made here. I declare there will always be a ball on this day to commemorate the time we held back the cursed horde!"

Cheers filled the air, and I glanced around to find Roger.

**"Still in his room,"** Grace said.

**"He's not doing anything but coming to terms with your revelation."**

Lord Adrijian finished his speech as I tried not to worry about Roger. The prospect of dinner was upon us all.

Everyone dished up themselves. It was a strange sight to see, as the narrator, watching my characters and filler characters acting how they should. I didn't sense any evil plot among them. They came together as Vaywell residents, enjoying a party at their Lord's manor house. I watched my world continue to move on, however out of hand it had become. These people were mine, and they weren't running for their lives. My story was salvageable, and I'd gotten a good chunk of words done. I just needed to keep going.

And get Tara and Paldric to fall deeper in love. An authentic love.

**"I'd wager a second tea party with Nora that we can get Tara and Paldric to kiss tonight,"** Grace said.

Really? Do you think so?

**"Are you talking about Andrea's little girl?"** Jim asked.

**"Of course! I would not wager a coveted invitation to a tea party hosted by the delightful Nora without some serious faith in our collective abilities."**

Alright, then. Let's get that second invitation to Nora's tea party.

# Chapter Thirteen

# THE WORK TO SECURE THE TEA PARTY INVITATION

The best I could do was stay out of Paldric and Tara's way. I sat near them during dinner, listening to them reminisce about their childhood. Two weeks ago, Tara added nothing to the conversation, just hanging on every word Paldric said. Now she was far more developed. The woman actually had memories to share with him. Memories of her father, who was always sick. The healer who could never heal himself. Back in book one, I casually told her she was an orphan, so I didn't have to deal with living parents. As I heard her pain about needing to be the town healer at fourteen so she could survive, I felt bad going with the default answer.

And Paldric, the man who believed everything worked out for the better, finally brought down the walls and admitted how much he missed his parents. How excited he was to explain the crazy adventure he'd been on. He wished they were here with him tonight, and the ache that was always there grew. His parents weren't fleshed out characters, but I might as well do that now. I closed my eyes, thinking.

"My mother adored my father," Paldric said in response to my thoughts. "They were an inseparable team. Honestly, if it wasn't for my mother's goodness, my father would have been disappointed in me."

Tara cut her pork into smaller pieces, but looked up, surprised. "Disappointed in you? That can't be true."

"I honestly think it is. My father, my grandfather, my great-grandfather, all incredible hunters. And I just... wasn't. I'm not very good. And I overheard my father talking it out with my mother multiple times, and she was always there to remind him I was more than my skills, or lack of them. Even though I wasn't good at hunting, I had other talents."

"Like bringing a town together to fight off goblins," Tara said.

Paldric about took a bite of pork, but lowered it. "Did I?"

Tara shook her head, smiling. "It wasn't that long ago."

"Seems like forever."

An entire book can feel like that, but I wouldn't tell them.

"Well, it's an admirable quality," Tara said.

"You're a good mix of your father and mother," Alwin said. I didn't intend for Alwin to join the conversation, but then again, he knew Paldric's parents.

"Really?" Paldric asked.

Alwin nodded. "You have so much of your mother's goodness. Everyone knew if you needed a smile, you went to—" I frowned, realizing I hadn't even given Paldric's mother a name. I dashed through a list of names, closing my eyes to concentrate. "You went to Catarina." I let out a breath, impressed by how fast I pulled that name out. "She would tell you stories, fill you with hope and a good meal, and you felt like your problems weren't nearly as hard as you thought. Not that she made you forget your problems. She simply had this way of making you understand it would be alright." Yep. That was absolutely Paldric. "And yet you are your father. You have Don's determination, his need to protect. If there is danger, he's the first one with his sword out. He commands, he leads. It's the primary trait of the men in your family. Yes, your family are known as hunters, but everyone in Omosa knew the actual skill they had was leadership."

Warmth blossomed in Paldric's chest, the kind he always felt as a child. The safety, the security, the thing he thought he'd never feel again because his parents were gone, but he had Alwin. The elf who knew his parents almost better than he did since he watched his father grow up.

Which made my narrator senses tingle: Alwin was probably going to die. Main characters needed to grow, and growth came from a healthy dose of suffering.

I stuffed the feeling down. It couldn't happen now, because I wasn't in complete control of my story. Besides, I already established he was, in his own way, an asexual and aromantic. I couldn't kill him, even if I wanted to. Can't bury your gays. Or your asexuals.

Doubt persisted, though. He wasn't asexual, humans just didn't attract him sexually.

Was I justifying my thought of killing him? No, I couldn't. None of my characters would die. Not while the Rogue Narrator was here. Alwin was safe.

Pretty sure.

"Alwin!" A random, filler character woman ran up to him. "The dance is starting! Let's go!"

"Oh, yay! I want to see the orchestra." Alwin stood up and headed toward the manor house, ignoring the actual reason the woman wanted Alwin to come with her.

I smiled to myself. The small orchestra played, and despite the chatting Paldric and Tara had before, they fell silent as they finished their dinner. Tara placed her utensils down. "Do you know how to dance, Paldric?"

"Not well."

"Could you teach me, anyway? I never had time to attend town gatherings."

He smiled and stood. "As long as you don't mind learning how to not dance well."

She smiled and took his hand, letting him help her find her footing with the heels before they walked to the makeshift dance floor. I finished my dinner, watching the gathering. There was still no sign of Roger.

**"Still in his room,"** Grace said.

I nodded, then stood, trying to find the best place to watch. I was more of an observer than a participator. It was the very definition of a narrator.

The sun had fully set, and the stars appeared in the night sky. I watched the door, waiting for Roger. Alwin listened to the orchestra with a crowd of women gathered around him as he kept talking about the fascinating instruments. Milla finally tugged on his sleeve and whispered that all these women wanted to dance with him. Sheepishly, he obliged.

Tara and Paldric were lost in their own world, doing the dances as well as they could. Neither cared that they made mistakes. Or giggled. Or looked at each other. A lot.

**"Suggest they go on a walk. Their chemistry right now is such that they'll be kissing before the grass becomes sand,"** Grace said.

Despite never seeing Roger come out the door, I still scanned the crowd for him. I left my spot as the song ended, heading toward them.

**"Roger is in his room, pacing now. According to the code, he's being inundated with the desire to leave his room and join the party,"** Jim said.

That was enough for me. I hurried over to Tara and Paldric. "Beautiful night, isn't it?"

"It is," Tara said as Paldric glanced up at the star covered sky. "Let's go for a walk. It's getting warm."

I watched them leave before following at a respectful distance.

**"Roger's walking out of his room,"** Grace said. My heart rate quickened, and I glanced at the door. **"I don't think it's for ill intent."**

**"Get some more ball descriptions in there. You can do it."**

I nodded, then glanced behind me. The outside ball was a pleasant sight to see. There was a whirl of colors and fabrics, greens, blues, and golds. The music played sweetly in the air, becoming a nice backdrop as Paldric and Tara walked toward the beach. The laughter at the ball was contagious, which was needed. Every so often, the face of a man dropped as he'd look at his family, knowing they'd leave tomorrow. A woman held her eldest son a little longer, trying to smile as she always did for her child, who was no longer a baby. Now old enough to protect her.

A lump appeared in my throat. I didn't want anyone to die in the battle ahead, but I couldn't do that without using my powers. I focused on Tara and Paldric again. She grabbed his arm, admitting she was terrified of taking a nasty fall in the heels she wore. Paldric, always the gentleman, wrapped his arm around her waist to steady her.

Roger appeared at the doorway right as I slipped past the lantern light. I stayed in the semi-darkness, watching all of them. Tara talked about the beautiful starlight, and Paldric said nothing, smiling at her. Tara saw his smile, then reached up and gave him a kiss, right where the sand met the grass.

Nice.

I crept farther into the darkness, trying to balance the need to monitor Paldric and Tara while also giving them whatever privacy they needed. My eyes leapt back and forth from Paldric and Tara to Roger. Despite what I figured out about him earlier, he was still someone I could not predict. I didn't know what the Rogue Narrator had planned when Roger saw Paldric and Tara.

Roger walked around the makeshift ball floor, his face stoic. He passed laughing couples, little brothers dancing with their little sisters, elderly couples, and acted as though they didn't exist. The contagious laughter that was such a blessing to those struggling with the uncertain future did not work on Roger. He walked through the crowd as though he was already on a battlefield.

He reached the banquet table, picking up a plate, filling it with his dinner. When he reached the end of the table, he glanced up to see Tara and Paldric. The two were still going strong in their make-out session, their arms wrapped around each other, their lips beginning to explore other places. Roger focused back on his food, which is when I concluded I was wrong to obsess about this becoming a love triangle.

**"Devin will be happy to hear that,"** Jim said.

I tried to smile, but then Roger sat down at a large, empty table with his back to Tara and Paldric, and I found I couldn't do it. I had treated Roger with less respect than he deserved, and I felt an obligation to check on him.

# Chapter Fourteen

# THE ROGUE NARRATOR PROVES HE HAS BETTER STEM SKILLS

I grabbed the seat across from Roger, one where I could still watch Tara and Paldric. Well, not watch them; I just wanted to keep them from danger. They were definitely not paying attention to their surroundings now.

The silence between me and Roger needed to end, and I should be the one to do it. "Hello."

Roger studied his plate like it was the most interesting thing in Veniloria. "Hello."

The back of the chair dug into my shoulder. The long grass poked my legs. Everything seemed to demand I notice it instead of keeping the conversation going, but I ignored it all except Roger. "What I said earlier this evening... what you've discovered about me..."

The man said nothing, simply pushed around his fork to gather some food before stuffing it in his mouth. I didn't know what to say, because giving words of comfort wasn't a strong suit of mine. Which is weird, considering my job as a narrator meant I survived on words making sense.

It came down to control. I controlled both sides of the conversation, and in the editing process, I could fix things to make it run smoother. It also caused me to see how horrible first drafts always were. Talking was just spewing first drafts left and right, and those always sucked. If I knew what Roger wanted to say, I could spend a few minutes crafting the perfect response, but I couldn't.

I cleared my throat, trying again. "I seemed to have misjudged your character, and I'd like to apologize."

"A lot more of our interactions have made sense in hindsight, that's for sure." Roger took another bite of dinner.

His words caused me to flinch. "I thought you were evil. I never thought the... the evil God would simply make you a..." Roger glanced up, finally meeting my gaze. "Make you kind. And considerate. And... good."

"If an evil God created me, does that not make me inherently evil? Can an evil God create something good?"

If Roger really needed an impromptu philosophical and religious discussion, then I'd muscle through it. At least he was talking.

"I think it's difficult to... to say evil, when there's clearly so much about that God we don't understand. Evil is just... just the word we use because..." Roger looked morbidly curious to see how I'd finish that sentence.

**"You're understanding how he's reacting,"** Jim said.

Well, I mean, how would you describe that face?

**"If you get to know him, you could predict how he'd react. You wouldn't need us to translate. It'd be helpful,"** Jim said.

I hadn't thought of that, or maybe I had, but briefly. If Jim and Grace could get a feel for my characters, I could do the same for the Rogue Narrator's creation.

Roger moved his food around his plate. "So, you're saying I'm not created by an evil God, just a misunderstood one that—that created goblins? And trolls? And a Dark Wizard? Who are all headed here to slaughter every man, woman, and child they can find?"

It was getting late, and I was tired. I had to think before trying to answer his question, and I took off my glasses to rub my eyes.

"Are your glasses bothering you?"

I glanced up, frowning at Roger's blurry outline. "You know what these are?"

He ate another bite. "Yeah. They help you see better."

My look turned critical as I returned my glasses to my nose. "You know someone else who wears them?"

He about answered, but froze. His frown deepened, as did his confusion. "No one. I know no one else who wears glasses. But I know what they are." He shrugged. "What a strange..." His fork clattered onto the plate as he touched his head. "What an odd..."

"Roger?"

**"Oh. Oh no,"** Jim said.

What's going on?

**"Screenshot it, Jim!"**

"Sorry. Got a headache all the sudden." He dropped his other utensil and used both hands to rub his forehead.

Nausea hit me, and I sat up straighter. "A headache? Like... like a pressure in your head?"

**"No!"** Jim said.

"Yes," Roger said at the same time, even though he couldn't have heard Jim. He picked up his fork again. "It's gone now, though."

**"Did you get it?"** Grace asked.

**"It was over too fast. Barely a flicker. I didn't have time."**

**"It's all right, dear."**

I stared at Roger, trying not to react, but I was a narrator, not an actor. Fear bubbled up inside me.

Jim? Grace? What should I expect?

Grace's calm voice did nothing for my nausea. **"I'm scrolling through Roger's code now, but I don't see any... no, wait. There's one sloppily buried here."**

The chair almost toppled over as I stood, trying to sense the code. There was nothing there, and it fed into my fears. Roger looked confused as I pointed at him. "The headache. What did it feel like?"

The stoic nature returned, but his eyes focused. "Like a... pressure."

"Did you sense anything with the pressure? Some sort of... code?" I tried out the modern word on his ears.

"Code?" Roger was at first confused, but looked at his plate again. "It... it felt like a probe. Does that make sense?"

"It does, yes. Do you feel any different?" I asked.

"No, no, not that I'm aware. Should I?"

**"We'll get it, just another minute,"** Jim said.

My mind was a haze of anticipation, but I went straight for my biggest fear. "Do you want to kill me?"

The stoicism melted, and Roger looked surprised. "What? No. Why would I do that?"

"In my defense, you already tried it earlier this evening."

"That was a warning. I don't kill men simply because I can." I could almost sense his realization, like he was one of my own characters. "Would the Rogue force me to do that?"

"Rogue." My heart hammered in my chest. "You said Rogue. You didn't say evil God."

Again, he looked confused. "It's who he is, isn't he? Isn't that... his name?"

"More his nom de plume." Roger nodded, my words making sense to him. "Tell me everything you can about what happened. Tell me anything you know about the Rogue. Anything at all."

"I... I..." Roger winced, rubbing his head again.

Is the code back?

**"No. He's trying to remember something,"** Jim said.

"Dissatisfied. That's the best way I can explain the emotion I felt during my headache. But I don't know what he's dissatisfied with. He's been doing this far too long and..." Roger rubbed his head again before shaking his head.

**"The Rogue Narrator is stopping him from digging much further,"** Grace said.

"Sorry. I don't know what else I can add." I gasped and grabbed the table's edge, clutching my chest. Roger stood, alarmed. "Gunther?"

An intense feeling of dread hit me. It was hard to breathe. Panic seized me as I looked at the guests. Something bad was going to happen. I sensed it in the code. The last time I sensed something like this...

**"Shadow soldiers. All of them. Headed straight for you,"** Jim said.

But that was impossible. The army is still days away, and the shadow soldiers can't travel long distances. Not unless...

My eyes shot toward the sky. There was no moon. No moon made them stronger, the shadows darker, and gave them the power to travel farther. A thing that only happened about once a month, and somehow it happened now, on the night of the ball. My stomach churned, and despite the level of fear in my heart, one self-deprecating truth settled on the surface. The Rogue Narrator was better at math than me.

Grace's usual gentle voice had a touch of edge to it. **"Get everyone inside. They won't travel in the light. Go inside, light all the lanterns you can."**

**"Roger was the beacon. They're coming. Fast."**

I pointed at Roger as I moved around the table to get Paldric and Tara. "Get everyone inside, now."

"What's going—"

Tara's scream cut Roger off. My neck popped with how fast my head snapped in her direction. Dark shadows snatched her waist and ripped her from Paldric's arms.

"No, no, no, no, no." It'd take too long to move around the table, so I just leapt over it, sprinting toward her.

"Tara!" Paldric shouted, scrambling after her.

Shadow soldiers popped up all over, swords out, beginning their slaughter. All our preparations for digging the moat seemed pointless now.

**"There are over five hundred in the area,"** Grace said.

Every single one. This was bad. A villain was supposed to send a frightening amount, but not so much to overwhelm the hero. But of course, the Rogue Narrator wouldn't care. He wasn't secretly on the side of my heroes. He wanted me to go insane, so he sent every shadow soldier straight for us.

The soldiers dragged Tara across the lawn, the beautiful white silk gown getting muddy and stained. Paldric pulled out his sword as we raced after them. Tara attempted to shove her heels into the ground to slow them down before she pulled out a dagger from... honestly, somewhere. I couldn't tell in the dark. I was just happy she came prepared as she slammed the point of the blade against one of the soldier's arms. It slowed them down enough that Paldric leapt forward with his sword, hacking away at the rest. The soldiers were impossibly fast, surrounding Paldric, Tara, and I.

Oh, this was bad.

**"Don't use your powers. Your percentage is way too high,"** Jim said.

It would be so easy, though. Forcing the sun to rise, make it day again.

**"Listen to what you're saying. There is nothing simple about making the sun rise right now,"** Grace said.

Paldric ran deeper into the horde as I helped Tara to her feet, and my heart froze. Yes, my main character would run into a horde of shadow soldiers, because that's who he was. I needed to help, but had no weapon. Nothing but—

"Don't." Tara grabbed my arm and pointed her dagger at me. "Don't even try it. Something that drastic will push you over the edge."

"With five hundred shadow soldiers here, you're somehow pointing that dagger at me?" I asked.

"Yes." Her voice never wavered, her eyes full of mistrust. "They're not as dangerous as you. Stand aside and let us handle it."

"What part of 'five hundred shadow soldiers' did you not understand?"

The blade was steady, still pointed at me. "And what part of 'you are more dangerous' did *you* not understand?"

I couldn't argue with her, because she was right. Tara glanced around, holding a dagger out toward some of the shadow soldiers headed straight for her. They had pale faces, yet the shadows that naturally fell were stark black. They had swords out, and Tara was ill prepared with a dagger. I remembered the fight with the goblins, and how they all came after me with their swords. It was fine when it was just me, but with Tara here, they would slaughter her. I couldn't let this happen. Not to Tara. I needed to *do* something.

Which is when light filled the night sky. Tara shot a look at me, horrified that I used some power, but another couple of seconds would have told her it wasn't me. My percentage wasn't rising. Besides, the light was more, uh, blue?

The soldiers surrounding us turned at this new threat, and I glimpsed Alwin. The sword and shield in his hands glowed with elven magic as he headed straight for the horde.

Oooh, this was going to be epic.

# Chapter Fifteen

## TEAM ALWIN!

Paldric was still alive, that much I could sense. He struggled with the shadow soldiers, as they were fast, but Alwin didn't waste time. His weapons were like two dim flashlights, but in the surrounding darkness, those flashlights were a blessing. The sword gleamed as he slashed at the soldiers. Even the smallest nick from the blade caused them to dissolve to the ground.

This might actually work without me using any powers.

"Tara. Find Milla and make sure everyone gets inside. Light all the lanterns and candles you can. They want to kidnap you," I said.

Tara brushed the dirt off her skirt as she moved, her eyes darting around the guests to find the little girl. I took a moment to consider the situation. Jim? Grace? Do you have any other information?

**"Alwin is your best bet. That is powerful magic, and the shadow soldiers are dropping like flies,"** Jim said.

My elf practically danced, the bodies around him dissolving into nothingness. He was on a mission to kill all five hundred. Paldric was somewhere deeper among the horde, making sure Alwin didn't have to kill all of them. The bluish gray glow of the sword was enough to see the vast number surrounding them. Alwin, undeterred, leapt from soldier to soldier, dropping them fast. Despite Alwin's inhuman ability to dodge blades, he would need all the help he could get.

**"And... right here. Milla is inside already with many other women and children,"** Grace said.

I grabbed Tara's wrist. "Get inside. Milla's already there. Stay in the light."

As though hearing me, a group of shadow soldiers turned on us, sneering before sinking into the ground. My heart leapt to my throat as I tightened my grip over her wrist. The shadows morphed and vibrated in the dim light of the moonless sky, making every hair on my body stand up at the sheer unnaturalness coming toward us. We backed away. Tara just had her dagger, and I only had sanity cracking God powers. I searched the ground for a sword to steal, but there were no bodies. And their swords disappeared once they died. I doubted my fists would be much good.

Despite my tight grip over Tara's wrists, someone ripped her away. I panicked for half a second before I saw Roger holding her. Then my panic shifted, and I felt helpless. Was Roger still good?

It happened fast. Roger arranged his grip over Tara, so it forced her to cling to him, her legs wrapped around his lower half. She shrieked in surprise, but didn't fight him. He pinned her waist to his side with one hand and held a sword in the other as he blocked the blows of three shadow soldiers partially raised from the ground.

Tara was slipping, but tried to hang on without throwing Roger off. "Roger! What are you doing?"

"They travel by shadow! If I set you down, they can grab you again. If you're not on the ground, they'll have to come through me." Roger kept fighting off the shadow swords that glowed purple.

Something told me Roger knew better than I did about shadow soldiers. I tried punching a shadow soldier, which wouldn't kill them, but it was better than nothing. My fist hit the soldier, and he stumbled right into Roger's blade, his essence melting to the ground. Roger and I glanced at each other, and I had to admit that was pretty cool.

He made quick work of the surrounding soldiers, waiting for a lull before lowering Tara to the ground. "I'm sorry. I don't know why, but these soldiers are drawn to you."

Tara tried to fix her hair. Uh... Jim? Grace? Did either of you describe her hair?

**"Nope. Go for it, Gunther,"** Grace said.

I thought maybe...

Somehow, I could hear Grace smiling. **"Don't feel intimidated. It's just hair."**

Did I have time to describe Tara's hair? Maybe I was thinking too hard about this.

At the beginning of tonight, Tara used pins to hold up her curls on top of her head. After shadow soldiers dragged her away, her curls fell to one side, and she hastily tried to brush them away from her face so she could see better.

That wasn't too hard. Wait, how did she curl her hair in a medieval fantasy novel? There are no curling irons.

**"We always find ways. Curling irons aren't the only way to get curls,"** Grace said.

Shadow soldiers swarmed toward a figure I sensed was Alwin. How many soldiers are left, Jim?

**"Give me a moment."**

Roger appeared beside me, pulling out a short sword and handing it over. I took it, thanking him, before we started hacking through the shadow soldiers.

**"About three hundred and fifty left. The other men are fighting as well. Do not crack."**

Got it.

Tara, Roger, and I hacked away at the horde. If it wasn't for my invulnerability, I'd already be dead. The soldiers split between Alwin and me, as though they knew we were the most important. If I wasn't careful, the soldiers would surround me again.

I let the shadow soldiers ease me away from the rest of the group. If my characters (and Roger) weren't next to me, they might be safer. Roger was next to Tara, fighting off the horde, and I could only hope he wouldn't get directions from the mysterious code.

Once the shadow soldiers surrounded me, they then sank to the ground. I panted, holding the hilt of the short sword in my hand as I looked around, confused, waiting for them to keep fighting.

Tara and Roger looked just as puzzled when the soldiers sank to the ground. I held the short sword close, knowing this was a trap. Of course it was. The Rogue Narrator wouldn't send every soldier at me, then take them away. That's something *I* would do to help my characters out at the last moment and drive up tension. The Rogue Narrator was not that kind of villain. He wanted us dead, no matter the cost.

In the heat of the battle, I didn't notice Alwin and Paldric had gone back-to-back, fighting off the horde. They remained that way for a moment longer, because they also sensed a trap. The two of them worked well together. No wonder they could have taken on a dragon in the first book.

Paldric kept his hand over the sword, prepared. "Everyone head back to the manor house nice and slow."

The silence stretched on between us, my fingers gripping the hilt of the sword as we headed to the house, trying not to turn our backs on anything. Roger slowly lowered his sword, keeping his eyes peeled. "You're great with that dagger."

Tara held it in both hands. "Thank you. I've been practicing."

He tore his gaze from the quiet battlefield to look at her for a bare moment before going back to studying every shadow. "I can tell. How long? A few months?"

"About a week."

He raised an eyebrow. "You have skill. I'll remember you can hold your own next time."

She spent the evening making out with Paldric and yet had the audacity to giggle at Roger. Okay, maybe not the whole night, but I could sense the "like Roger" aspect of her character deepening. It was enough for my eyes to narrow, which meant I didn't pay attention.

A shadow soldier popped right next to Tara and thrust his sword toward her gut. Roger, however, pushed her aside. The shadow soldier redirected and instead stuffed his sword into Roger's chest, which caused my body to stop working.

Alwin shouted, running straight for them. The soldier threw his sword at Alwin, who easily stepped aside before stabbing him with his blue-gray sword, causing him to dissolve.

"Roger?" The healer in her tried to stay calm, but she considered Roger a friend, and it was difficult to not reveal the fear in her voice.

Paldric sprinted forward, sheathing his sword. I grabbed Roger's arm to keep him steady. He wasn't looking at the wound in his chest, his face hard to read, though considerably paler. Roger's knees gave out right as Paldric grabbed him. "No, no, no," Paldric said.

The man couldn't speak. Almost like he didn't want to. I racked my brain, searching for anything I knew about Roger's character. He wasn't about to break down and cry in front of everyone, but then again, the hole in his chest was draining blood at an alarming rate. Roger might be experiencing shock.

**"He doesn't have long,"** Jim whispered.

Tara forced herself to gain control of her fear. She stood up, pointing at Paldric. "Get him into the manor house now. We can't stay out here in the dark with those shadow soldiers. I'll see what I can do."

Alwin got on the other side of Roger and helped lift him. We ran, me in the back of the group, keeping Roger's short sword out. The grounds were still too quiet, except for the other men bringing in their wounded.

We met Lady Ana at the door as she rushed us into a guest room. Paldric and Alwin set Roger on the bed before tearing open his shirt. I had balked earlier at the idea of Tara seeing him shirtless, but everyone had to admit the nasty hole in his chest was far more distracting. I had to turn away, bile creeping up my throat. Tara had her pack, pulling out a cloth to press against the wound. Roger let out a deep groan before his eyes rolled to the back of his head.

**"The shadow soldiers have retreated. None of them remained,"** Grace said.

That's ridiculous. The Rogue Narrator wouldn't do this. He'd keep them coming until I cracked. He still has three hundred soldiers at his disposal and wants this world destroyed.

**"And yet they're gone. Since Roger's dying, something tells me this is what the Rogue Narrator wants,"** Jim said.

But why? It makes no sense. That's something *I* would do if I was controlling the villain. He sent every single shadow soldier out here. Why isn't he trying to murder everyone?

Tara ordered Paldric to hold the cloth against Roger's chest as she opened one of her bottles. She held the back of Roger's head, trying to tip the bottle to force something into his mouth. The liquid hit his unresponsive lips, trickling down the side of his chin. Tears filled her eyes. "He's got to be alright. He saved me, so I've got to save him."

**"Wait, the Rogue Narrator never murders like this. Not this cleanly."**

What are you saying, Jim?

**"He only murders if he knows it'll alter your characters beyond what they can handle. Or, in this case, if it adds to your cracking."**

Paldric touched Tara's arm, compassion filling his expression. "I know it's hard, but he'd rather it be this way."

"No." Tara didn't look at him. Instead, her eyes shot to me, standing near the doorway. "Heal him, Gunther."

# Chapter Sixteen

# PROS AND CONS OF DEATH

My face dropped. "Sorry, what?"

"Heal him." Tara repeated it like it would answer all my questions if she simply asked again.

I placed the short sword on the top of a dresser. "You know better than anyone why I can't do that."

Tara handed the bottle to Paldric before walking over to me, glaring. "I know you, yes. I know what I said. You don't want to heal him, therefore it won't be as big of a spike."

"That's not... what? I'd be using my God powers. Of course it would take a chunk out of my percentage."

"No, it won't. The information is coming to me right now." She waved at her head. "Whoever Roger is, he's someone you don't want to heal. If you use your God powers for selfish reasons, like if this was Paldric, there'd be a fifteen or twenty percent jump. But with Roger it's only a percent. One small percent."

Jim? Grace? Tara's just grief stricken, right? There's no way this could work.

**"Hard to tell. Keep staring at her to get information,"** Jim said.

My brows furrowed, trying to pull the secret out. Tara stared right back, hands on her hips, letting me sense the information freely. She believed what she said. The part she didn't tell me about was the gamble. Using my God power could also make me want to heal the other injured men. Though the Guardians liked to lump the God-power as selfishly inclined, there was nuance to it. Doing something I didn't want to do wouldn't hurt my percentage too much. But if healing Roger instead inspired me to heal everyone else, that would hurt my percentage.

How many injured men were there?

**"Thankfully no casualties, but some pretty nasty bumps and bruises,"** Grace said.

"Tara..."

She did not let me finish. "Please, Gunther. Please heal him."

"Is it true?" Paldric's face lit up with hope. "Can you heal him with only a little percentage rise?"

I stared at Paldric, feeling nauseous. He wanted me to heal Roger, because of course he did. If there was some good to be done in the world, Paldric would suggest it without question. I, on the other hand, had questions.

Tara pointed to Roger. "He saved my life. He has proved his true character! So, heal him!"

Alwin leaned over Roger, listening to his breathing. "Healing his injuries may just be one percent, but what about bringing him back to life? He doesn't have much time."

"It's not much of a difference." Tara still looked at me with hard eyes.

My frown deepened. "Don't lie, Tara. I can't bring Roger back to life without a three percent increase."

"Still a lot smaller than if you did the same thing to Paldric."

I pointed to my head. "And we cannot afford that right now. My sanity is over fifty percent. I can't let it rise at all."

"Please, Gunther!" Tara said.

My heart pounded in my chest as I glanced at Roger again. His own heart was sorta in his chest. There was blood everywhere. *Everywhere.* Roger's eyes were closed, and I couldn't detect his breathing.

There was no way I could risk this. They didn't know what they were asking of me. No, wait, Tara knew. She understood exactly what this might do, and yet she still looked at me with pleading eyes.

The room had a coppery smell that I tried to ignore, but once I thought about ignoring it, it hit my senses in full force and I gagged. Once the nausea passed, I dropped my hand. "He still has an embedded..." I trailed off. How could I communicate this to my characters? "He has a hidden personality deep inside him that could make him turn on all of us." They looked at me, none of them getting it. "His character is one way but could change to be another, more evil type."

"Are you certain it might be an evil personality?" Paldric asked.

"Considering it's from the evil God, pretty certain," I said, trying and failing to keep the dryness from my voice.

"But do you have any proof?"

Paldric wasn't asking the correct questions. It was enough to make me stare. "No, I don't have proof."

Tara placed a hand on Roger's bare shoulder. "This man will die if you don't do something."

I wanted to rip her hand off his shoulder and almost did. Instead, I curled my fingers in and pressed my fist to my mouth. "Yeah, well, he did just get stabbed through the chest with a sword. Got to think about natural consequences." The words barely made it past my fist.

My thoughts were jumbled and unfocused. If I heal Roger right now, I would raise a percentage. But if I waited until after he died, there would be a three percent jump. But did I want to heal him? Despite my characters begging me to, I still didn't know if it was worth it. I couldn't think. Everything was happening too fast.

**"Grace, you're pros, I'm cons. Go,"** Jim said.

**"The biggest pro I'm seeing to healing Roger is your characters won't hate you. Tara and Paldric are both adamant you do this. If you don't, it will be a difficult thing to regain their trust."**

**"The story never depended on whether they like you. It depends on them remaining in character until the end of the book. And one percent is no joke right now."**

They were talking fast for my benefit. I didn't know how long we had until Roger was dead, but it couldn't be long.

**"Gunther already established in book one that Tara's character could alter because of how much she hated him. If they hate him enough, it could play into the Rogue Narrator's hands,"** Grace said.

**"Nevertheless, we don't know the embedded code in Roger. That is still a concerning mystery. If Gunther saves Roger, the rest of them might die or get tortured beyond recognition,"** Jim said.

**"Roger was actively trying to help Gunther figure out who the Rogue Narrator is. That is a valuable quality right now, and someone worth having around."**

Grace was right. Despite my initial distrust of Roger, that was a quality that had an allure to it. An idea struck me. I pointed at Paldric. "Does it bother you that Roger could kill you?"

"No." I knew he wouldn't mind. My main character knew, deep down, things always turned out for the best.

"Does it concern you he might kill anyone else if he stays alive? Tara? Alwin?" I took a deep breath. "Milla?"

Paldric hesitated, glancing at Tara. She frowned, realizing the full impact of this choice. She then shook her head. "That doesn't seem like Roger. He wouldn't kill Milla."

"But if he does? Would you be able to handle it if Roger murdered Milla once I brought him back?" I asked.

Tara and Paldric shared another glance before he turned back to me. "We would see her again in the database, right?"

It surprised me Paldric remembered the database and pronounced it so well. True, the "afterlife" would be impossible to forget, and he gained a lot of comfort from it.

"You will, yes," I said.

"This is the right thing to do. If you can heal him, you should," Paldric said.

Alwin frowned. "What's a database?"

I turned to Alwin, the cynical one. Well, if you take me out of the group, then he is. I sort of took over that role when I arrived, but Alwin's opinion was still important.

"I'll explain the database later. Should I heal Roger? Are you willing to take the consequences from it?"

My elf watched me closely, and I saw his thought process. He was numb to the idea of death. He saw much of it in his one hundred and fifty years of existence. But he still risked revealing his elf nature not only to the evil army but also to the people of Vaywell to protect his friends. He would do everything to protect this group that had accepted him.

And that included Roger.

It seems I am outvoted.

**"Honestly, I'm glad you think godhood is a democracy. Might help you last,"** Jim said.

I'm not writing this story for myself. This story is for them. It always has been. To give them a chance to live and be who they are.

I really hope I don't regret this.

Tara let go of Roger as I grabbed his shoulder, healing him in an instant before death took him. All the blood fled back into his body, and the hole in his torso snapped shut. Roger sat up, clutching his chest, breathing like he finally realized how and was making up for the lack of air.

"Fifty-four," Tara whispered. She grabbed his hand in a concerned manner. Because they were friends. That's all there was.

"Was this you?" Roger asked Tara between breaths.

Somehow, despite this miraculous healing, I was not the first person Roger assumed had helped him. And he was kind of right.

Tara shook her head before gesturing toward me. Roger frowned. "You?"

I waited for some emotion to play across his face, but he clutched his chest, staring at me with that stupid stoicism. Before I could stop myself, I let the words slip. "I was outvoted."

Even that barb elicited no response from him. His emotions would not reveal themselves so easily on his face.

My feet carried me toward the door. With no windows and plenty of light, they would remain safe from the shadow soldiers. I needed some fresh air. The coppery smell disappeared as soon as I used my powers, but I still felt nauseous. I kept the door open in case Roger did something, or, rather, the Rogue Narrator forced Roger to do something. My imagination conjured up an image of all my characters lying in a heap on the ground with Roger standing above them. I stayed close to the room, just in case.

**"You're solidly past thirty thousand words in the sequel, Gunther. You can leave whenever you want to. The book is almost halfway done,"** Jim said.

It wasn't nearly as comforting as Jim hoped it would be.

# Chapter Seventeen

# The Consequences of Life

Milla rushed toward me, and I wrapped my arms around her.

"What's going on?" The terror was clear in her face. "I saw you all bringing in Roger. Is he—" she swallowed, "—dead?"

I looked at my little eight-year-old character, realizing how much she'd gone through the past few weeks. Hopefully, she wouldn't have to go through much more.

"Roger's fine. He's alive."

Milla's face visibly relaxed, then broke into a smile. "Oh, good."

This little girl barely knew Roger, and yet she was attached to him. I saw her memories of when Roger had been so kind to her. He made sure she worked through the anxiety she felt about the monsters we faced. Something I should have done with her. Or even Paldric. We had been so busy the past couple of days; we neglected some bonding experiences with Milla, and it all went to the Rogue Narrator's character.

Roger, for as long as I've known him (which wasn't long), had been good. He, too, didn't have that weird TM symbol in front of Good Guy. If I didn't know about the secret code embedded in him, I, too, would have trusted his goodness. Except someone who actively wanted to harm my story created him, and I couldn't shake that. There was no way my guard would drop around him.

"You can go see him. Leave the door open," I said.

She nodded and rushed in. In her hurry to hug him, she thankfully left the door wide open, and I saw my characters (and the one everyone else wanted to save). Roger sat on the edge of his bed, rubbing his still bare chest where the sword wound used to be not that long ago. He smiled at Paldric and Tara, who checked up on him, making sure he was okay. Alwin handed Roger the short sword he gave me.

"Oh, thank you." Roger stood up to sheath it, Tara on the other side of him to make sure he was steady. After experiencing some of those miraculous healings myself before, the brain would be convinced it was still maimed.

Other than a slight stumbling of the feet, Roger seemed fine, and Tara kept a hand on him to make sure he was okay. His stoicism might not let me know how he truly felt, though.

Roger was still shirtless, but Tara didn't seem to notice. Yes, maybe I overreacted. Tara had slipped into the healer's role now and had seen plenty of unclothed humans, and there was nothing sexual about it.

As Roger put on a fresh shirt, Tara didn't even glance at his photoshopped eight pack (there was no way a guy could get eight abs). Instead, she smiled at Paldric and took his hand. It would take a lot more than a shirtless Roger to turn her head.

Which I should have trusted, but I'm the cynical one in this group.

Something rammed so hard against the manor house all of us took notice. Milla whimpered and backed into Roger, who lifted her up, holding on to her, whispering in her ear words of comfort.

More things rammed against the manor house, and the dread returned. We left the guest room and entered the dining hall where the rest of the injured city folk were. The room turned into a small hospital with many makeshift beds. Tara's mind turned to how she could help with bandages and oils before she focused on the pounding.

"What's happening?" Milla asked.

Alwin took out his sword. "The shadow soldiers are back and trying to get in."

Roger kept holding Milla. "We'll be fine as long as we don't leave this manor house. There's enough light here they can't come."

I turned toward Roger, half expecting him to grab us all and throw us out, but he simply met my gaze, the stoicism melting to reveal a curious look. I forced myself to look away.

Jim? Grace? How many shadow soldiers are left?

**"About three hundred. The Rogue Narrator sent every single one again, and those not tasked with breaking down the manor house are filling the moat back in."**

"Of course they are," I mumbled.

Alwin's scarred ears twitched. "What was that?"

I rubbed the bridge of my nose, my glasses bobbing up and down. "The ones not trying to attack are filling in the moat."

Paldric winced, giving his sore hands a fleeting glance.

"What do we do?" Roger asked.

A lot of my filler characters stared at Alwin, realizing exactly who he was. Alwin, who enjoyed being alone and ignored, would be the center of attention now. My elf's skill was in a class all its own, but this was three hundred shadow soldiers. We had barely survived killing two hundred.

Paldric unsheathed his sword, standing next to Alwin. "There are women and children in here. I cannot, in good conscience, wait for the threat to be over. If we kill as many as we can, there will be fewer enemies to fight in the coming days."

Roger patted Paldric on the back before taking out his own sword. "I agree. Three hundred shadow soldiers are easier to deal with than the entire Dark Wizard's army." He closed his eyes. "Not only that, but they could travel over the moat at nights during the battle, even with it being completed. We either fight them now, or later, when the army eventually gets here. I don't want to deal with them after fighting the goblins and trolls all day." He opened his eyes. "And I have something to prove."

Tara frowned, glancing at him. "You do?"

"Yes." Roger pulled out the short sword and handed it back to me, the emotions on his face difficult to read. "That I'm nothing like them."

Roger didn't call me out specifically, but it still felt like he did. It caused me to wince. It was clear I didn't trust him. I wanted everyone to stay inside so I could keep an eye on Roger, but once again, I was outvoted. My fingers wrapped around the hilt of the sword and gave a pathetic nod.

Grace? Jim? How much longer until the sun rises?

**"At least two hours. Almost three,"** Grace said.

Their idea was sound, except for Roger, the wild card. I rubbed my forehead, frowning. "Alright, Paldric and Alwin, stay together. Roger, stay with me. We cannot get surrounded again."

Fifty of my male filler characters approached. "This sounds like a good idea. We would like to join."

I ignored the clunky dialogue. They may be filler characters, but they were on our side.

One of them bowed to Alwin. "It would be an honor to fight with the Master Elf."

Alwin's face dropped. He knew leaping out into battle with the energized sword and shield would be a dead giveaway, but he still looked uncomfortable. For an elf, anyway.

Paldric gave Alwin a half hug. "We would love to have you men fight with us. These shadow soldiers won't catch us off guard again, and with our combined might, we will defeat them once and for all."

The men cheered, collectively deciding. I rubbed my forehead, the short sword feeling heavy in my hand. "If we're going to do this, we must go now. It's the only element of surprise we'll have. Truthfully, they already know we're coming."

Paldric and Roger frowned, but no one asked me questions. Tara grabbed Milla's hand. She was already planning on helping as a healer. There was plenty to do, and she wanted Milla to hold her pack of supplies to distract her from our mission. She asked the little girl some questions about how queasy she felt.

Roger stayed beside me as Paldric and Alwin slipped away to the other side of the house. I almost felt sick at the thought of them dying, but Alwin with the sword and shield helped me feel slightly better.

"Follow me, stay close," I told Roger as we moved out of the room.

He obeyed, falling into step next to me. I refused to meet his gaze, distracting myself by looking out the windows near the door to see if I could spy the shadow soldiers. About twenty-five men followed behind us. Roger leaned against the wall, rubbing his chest again, the only sign it was still bothering him.

"We've got to hit them where it hurts. And we've got to be fast," I said.

"Gunther—"

"We don't have time for a heart-to-heart. We've got to move while many of them are filling up the moat," I said.

Roger held his sword close, trying to see past the house. "I just wanted to say I know it wasn't your choice to heal me, but it would be a crime if I didn't thank you. I owe my life to you."

I glanced at the character that was not mine, once again confused. The Rogue Narrator made a sympathetic character, not a brooding bad boy, and it threw me off. "Um... you're welcome."

We didn't have time to say much more. We slipped out of the house, me, Roger, and the small band of men prepared to take on the shadow soldiers.

The air was clear. The ocean breeze picked up and ruffled our hair as we tried to move like elves, staying close to the house, searching the shadows. But they disappeared. We kept our swords out as we traveled the length of the house, running into Paldric, Alwin, and their group.

Paldric frowned, looking around. "Where'd they go?"

I lowered the short sword, glancing up at the moonless sky, the dread no longer filling me. A different sort of dread did. "They're gone."

"What? Why?" my main character asked.

My gaze returned to Roger. I didn't even have to incline my head, since he wasn't that much taller than me. I remembered what he said that inspired all of us to do this ridiculous mission. Killing all the shadow soldiers now would benefit us in the long run. Shadow soldiers could move past the moat at night, and we'd have to face them after fighting trolls and goblins all day. The Rogue Narrator must have liked the idea.

I handed Roger his short sword back, feeling defeated. Confused, he took it. "Gunther?"

"It's late. I'm going to bed." The full effects of the night drained me of adrenaline. "Wake me up before the women and children leave. I'd like to give Milla a proper goodbye."

Everyone watched as I made my way back into the manor house. Despite my exhaustion, I kept my thoughts to myself. I doubt they would've made much sense anyway.

# Chapter Eighteen

# Unreliable Narrators Cannot Be Trusted

I was eight years old, once. It was the first day of summer vacation and a beam of sunlight filled my room. My body woke up naturally. I was already smiling because my dream was full of adventure where none of the monsters scared me, and I defeated the bad guys. The smell of bacon filled the air, and I listened to it crisping in the pan. Bacon was the loudest noise, but I knew Mom was making chocolate chip pancakes like she promised. It was going to be a huge breakfast of eggs and hash browns, too. A feast fit to start the summer off right.

That perfect childhood morning became a litmus test for every morning since. The first day of summer vacation, no responsibilities, and a hot breakfast ready. It was the quintessential way to wake up.

Waking up with a dagger to my throat was the new litmus test of the worst ways to wake up.

"What's going on? Who are you?" I sputtered, wanting to move, but not daring. I squinted up at the figure not that far from my bed. No, figures. There were three of them. My characters. Tara was in the center, her dagger still poised at my throat. Alwin had his bow out, with an arrow set in the string, alarmingly pointed right at me. Paldric had his sword out, not pointing at me, but ready.

I slowly got up to rest on my elbows. "Does someone want to explain what's happening?"

"That's what we'd like to ask you." There was little emotion in Tara's voice. Paldric handed me my glasses, and I put them on my nose slowly because there were too many weapons pointed at me right now. "Why did your percentage jump three percent last night?"

My eyes bounced between the three of them. "Wait, what?"

"You're at fifty-seven percent. How did that happen? What did you do?" Tara's voice was now as sharp as the dagger pressed against my throat.

**"Gunther. Explain yourself now,"** Devin said.

"Three percent? Three…" I stared, bewildered. "I… I don't know. It must have been from the battle last night and healing Ro—" I was going to keep talking, but Tara placed her blade closer to my throat. Though it didn't physically cut me off, I assumed she wanted me to stop.

"Don't lie to me, Gunther. This had nothing to do with healing Roger."

Paldric reached forward, touching Tara's wrist to ease her dagger away from my throat. "Remember what we talked about?"

They spoke in code, but it was pointless. Just looking at my main character told me the three of them discussed things beforehand. Mostly that they couldn't get angry at me, especially Tara. It frightened Paldric that her fear might overtake her, and she'd try to kill me. Then I would defend myself, and it might spike my percentage again.

Tara narrowed her eyes, but eased the dagger away from my throat. "It wasn't the battle catching up with you. From what I understand, part of that percent spike was you using your powers to hide what you did from me."

**"Gunther,"** Devin hissed.

My confusion was legitimate. "I…I didn't… *what*?"

"I will only ask one more time." Tara raised her dagger to my chin so she could stare directly into my soul. "What did you do last night to cause this spike?"

My eyes remained on her before I glanced at Alwin, who kept his arrow aimed right between my eyes.

**"Answer the question, Gunther,"** Devin said.

"You're going to have to believe me," I whispered, both to my characters and to Devin. "I don't know how that spike happened. I'm just as concerned as all of you."

Tara hesitated, studying me, and I let her. There was nothing but truth in my eyes. She frowned as she sheathed her dagger. "Somehow, this was still you. I don't like it, but I will believe you. So let me repeat you are at fifty-seven percent, and it *cannot* rise anymore."

"Agreed." I didn't realize how shallow I'd been breathing until Alwin lowered his weapon. "Three percent is an insane jump for something I don't remember."

**"You must have forced yourself to forget it,"** Devin said.

What?

**"Like when you forgot about your name. But this time, whatever you did, you forced yourself to forget so you could tell Tara with a clear conscience you did nothing."**

What Devin said unsettled me far more than Tara's dagger at my throat. If I could do that to myself, then I needed to figure out what I did last night. This was the move of an unreliable narrator. Unreliable to myself.

"Um… is Roger okay?" I couldn't help but ask.

Paldric sheathed his sword. "He's fine. Still asleep, last I checked."

His words didn't comfort me. I sat up, placing my feet against the floor as I rubbed my head. My first fear was I killed Roger, but it would have caused more than a three percent jump. Possibly. I didn't know how much it would take to murder a character and then force myself to forget it.

"Depends on how you do it," Tara said.

I glanced at her, frowning. "Sorry?"

She matched my frown. "I don't know, I just…" Her frown deepened as she looked toward the ceiling. Information was coming to her as she thought about it. If I murdered a character without using powers and forced myself to forget, it might give me a five percent spike. If I murdered with powers and covered it up, that would be a good ten percent spike. None of the numbers added up to my own three percent.

Tara took out her dagger, about ready to press it against my throat again. "Why are you thinking about that?"

I raised my hands, trying to look innocent. "Morbid curiosity. I wanted to make sure I didn't do *that* last night. Clearly I didn't. The spikes don't match up."

Tara narrowed her eyes again, but believed me. Honestly, I'm just glad she didn't have access to my internet history while I was writing this book.

Not... not because of *that*. But because... because narrators always had odd search histories.

**"Yeah, I relate,"** Devin said.

My chest relaxed. At least Devin understood.

**"I laughed when Jim showed me his. How fast does blood drain the body when an artery is hit. The process of rigor mortis. Images of bodies dead after four hours. Then a thesaurus search for 'running'. We are an odd breed."**

Especially those murder mystery writers.

My smile remained as I stood, and my characters backed away from me. It probably didn't help that Tara knew I was thinking about murdering someone and then forgetting about it, all while having a smile on my face. I cleared my throat. "Alright, well." I rubbed my hands together, trying to not look like a psychopath. "This is an alarming development, so I thank you for bringing it to my attention." The three of them watched me like mice approaching a hawk's nest, and I couldn't blame them. I didn't know what else to do but stifle my smile, causing Tara to take a step back. "Um... breakfast? Shall we have breakfast?"

They agreed. In the dining hall, Tara sat next to me with her bowl of oatmeal. She did her best to hide a kitchen knife so I wouldn't notice, but also in a place she could grab it quickly if needed. The fact remained that she had a kitchen knife with her while we were all eating oatmeal. I pretended to ignore it.

Roger walked in, looking like he just woke up from barely any sleep. Given what happened last night, it was understandable.

I sipped my coffee, compliments of the illustrious island of Jimdon, and looked away as Roger sat across from me.

"Good morning, everyone. I hope you all slept well." Tara said nothing to Roger's greeting, still watching me. Alwin finished his breakfast, and Paldric sat next to Tara, almost like he was keeping *her* in check. Roger frowned. He must have picked up on the strange atmosphere. "What happened?"

"Nothing," I said at the same time Tara said, "Gunther spiked three percent."

Roger raised an eyebrow, looking at me. I sighed. It honestly didn't matter if he knew. The Rogue Narrator would already know, because he was following along in the story. I rubbed a small section above my eyebrow before smiling at Roger.

"Do you want to talk about it?" Roger asked.

"There's nothing to talk about. I don't remember why I spiked." I realized Tara had woken up Paldric to help check on me and ask what happened. Alwin needed little sleep, so he was already awake. "Why wasn't Roger part of the wake-up committee, Tara?" I asked, mostly out of curiosity.

"Because I didn't know how you'd react to Roger being in your room, pointing a weapon at you," Tara said.

I hesitated, then glanced at Roger. "Yeah. Okay. That's fair."

Maybe his stoicism didn't work early in the morning. Either way, I saw his hurt flicker plainly across his face. It surprised me.

**"According to the code you don't have access to, it stems from his comments last night. He doesn't want to be associated with the cursed creatures. Your constant mistrust is a reminder of his real creator, and it unnerves him."**

Roger looked away, working to get the stoicism back. Milla sat down next to him with her bowl of oatmeal. No one said anything. I waited for Tara to rat me out again, but a spike in my percentage was not something to divulge to an eight-year-old. Especially since she was about to leave with the other women and children.

Milla ignored everyone as she took a perfect bite of oatmeal. She even used a cloth napkin to dab the sides of her clean mouth. My spike made everyone else distracted enough that they didn't give Milla a second thought, which was better this way. Today was the day she executed her plan to stay here in Vaywell, and I made sure no one paid attention to Milla.

**"Why?"** Devin's voice was as full of suspicion as Tara's.

Because I'm right. Milla needs to stay with us. The second it gets dark, those shadow soldiers will kidnap her to draw us out.

**"Does this have something to do with what you forgot?"**

Possibly, but I doubt it. Milla has a plan already, and there's nothing I need to do other than make sure her plan is successful.

Milla finished in record time, dabbing her mouth again before standing. "I've got to go finish packing."

"Let me know if you need help," Tara said.

The little girl nodded before disappearing from the dining hall.

**"Gunther, we need to talk. Now."**

Yeah, what is it?

**"The chapter title just came in. Would you mind explaining it to me?"**

I swirled my spoon in the oatmeal, glancing around. What does the chapter title say?

**"Unreliable Narrators Cannot Be Trusted."**

True enough.

**"You're certain you remember nothing from last night?"**

My gaze met Tara's again, sensing the spike in my percentage. Three percent. What could have happened that caused a three percent spike?

**"Gunther?"**

I don't know, Devin. I honestly do not know.

# Chapter Nineteen

# Unspecific Chapter Title Placed Here

We finished breakfast and left the manor house. It was still early morning, and the women and children were preparing to leave. It made me uneasy that they were leaving after knowing the Rogue Narrator still had three hundred shadow soldiers. My nausea would've been worse if I knew Milla was joining them.

All of us took turns hugging Milla, wishing her well. I did enough to pass by, but Paldric and Tara lingered, making sure she'd be okay. I moved away, but not too far, just to make sure whatever they said wouldn't inspire her to go with the other women and children. She needed to stay, and her plan was solid.

**"Gunther, this chapter heading—"**

I already told you, Devin. I don't know what it means.

**"No, this is a new chapter now. And the title heading came in frighteningly fast. Unspecific Chapter Title Here. That's the title."**

Is it? That seems unusual.

**"Especially since we're starting a new chapter. They usually appear at the end. Did you order the device to do this?"**

What? No, of course not! This is starting to freak me out. I apparently can't trust myself or the device.

**"Alright, I didn't mean to make you panic. There's got to be a reason. Maybe the device is clueing us in to what you did."**

My fingers got tangled in my hair as I closed my eyes tight to forget this entire morning. No, not actually forget, since apparently I could do that, but I tried to focus on what mattered. Milla needed to execute her plan. She couldn't go with these women and children, or she would put them all in danger. The Rogue Narrator might attack this group with his shadow soldiers, but I doubted he would try without Milla there. He needed me and would focus all his energy on the characters that would break me if they died.

My eyes wandered to where the women and children were gathered. A woman hugged her husband in order to hide the fact that he was transferring a sheathed dagger into his wife's pocket to not frighten their children. A five-year-old boy burst into tears, holding his mother, and sobbed uncontrollably. The five-year-old's outburst caused many other children to lose their calm demeanors, and they cried, too. Many of them might never see their fathers and brothers again. Many of their fathers and brothers were simply praying to the moon that they weren't sending the women and children to their deaths.

I turned away, my throat constricting. This incredibly touching scene would not get to me. There was no way I would become this attached. The Rogue Narrator might kill them if he thought it would cause me to break faster. Therefore, I simply didn't react to this scene, so the Rogue Narrator would leave this group alone. I didn't care about their fate. Not as much as my main cast of characters.

"Papa! Papa, please!" a little girl screamed.

I slammed my hands around my ears to stop the noise that might make my heart crack. My eyes were wide as I stared at the sky. This story was doing a number on me.

**"They'll be fine. Your logic is sound. The Rogue Narrator is coming after you. As long as Milla stays in Vaywell, there is no reason for him to attack a group of fillers."**

The emotions kept my words hostage, but luckily with Devin, I didn't have to speak. He was right. By the evening, the women and children would be too far for the shadow soldiers to reach, since there would be a moon. The best thing I could do to keep them safe was to make sure Milla's plan worked. My main characters were the bigger target for the Rogue Narrator, and if Milla wasn't with them, he wouldn't attack the women and children. And speaking of...

Roger walked toward the manor house, and I jogged over before falling in step with him. "Oh, hello, Gunther."

"Hi Roger." I patted his shoulder, turning him away from the manor house. "Let's dig that moat."

"Yeah." He allowed me to pull him toward the moat. "That sounds like a better idea. I had the strangest feeling to stay in the manor house."

"What?" I let a small laugh escape me. "That *is* strange. Why would you stay here?"

"I don't know. That moat needs to be dug. Who knows how much longer we have until the army gets here?"

"Who knows, indeed." I sensed Milla watching Roger before giving her last hugs to Tara and Paldric. I didn't dare look at her, because I didn't want Roger's focus to shift toward her. "We need a powerful man like you to help dig. You did some incredible work yesterday."

"Not necessarily. I'm pacing myself so my hands wouldn't get blisters. That's the most important thi—"

Roger slowed to a stop, frowning. "Did I forget something back at the manor house?"

"No, of course not. What could you forget? They have all the tools on the beach. Come, we must get started." I did my best to not drag Roger out there.

He stopped, and I didn't dare do anything else but wait for the next excuse the Rogue Narrator would give me.

"I... I actually need to use the bathroom. In the manor house."

My face fell. Never, during all of book one, had any of my characters needed to use the bathroom. I had, admittedly, not developed the urinary needs of my characters, and there was most definitely no "bathroom" in the manor house.

"Uh..." Lessee, medieval fantasy, little running water. "You mean... you'd like to use the... chamber pot?"

"Yes," Roger said, like we were having a normal conversation about bodily functions. Which... okay, they were normal, but I never developed these functions for anyone else.

"That's great because... I do too." I sensed chamber pots appear in strategic places in the manor house far away from us. No, I didn't actually need to. The thoughts were never strong enough for the device to pick up. Pretty sure the doctors and nurses in my real life were taking care of my coma induced body and the functions I needed.

**"Yep,"** was all Devin said.

Book logic was illogical.

Roger received another pat on the back from me. "I'll come with you."

He gave me a weird look. "You want... to come with me? To use a chamber pot?"

I blinked a few times, trying to figure out how to be less of a creep. "When you've gotta go, you gotta go."

Roger still looked at me distrustfully, but we headed back to the manor house.

Okay, so I haven't researched the details about a chamber pot. Just that... they were in bedrooms? Pretty sure? This was clearly a ploy to get Roger back and searching in the manor house, so I had to foil it. I hurried to catch up with him, smiling as he kept giving me a weird look.

"I'll not go there with you. Just... use my own. In my little... room."

Roger wouldn't tell me I was making him uncomfortable. This could work to my advantage. The women and children were already leaving, and I hurried beside Roger so he wouldn't notice how slowly Milla walked.

I went to my room, keeping my door open. The instant Roger's door closed, I crept over and grasped the knob. I waited, my heart pounding. Milla's shadow fell across the hallway, and she covered her mouth to keep in a gasp when she saw me. I put a finger to my lips before ushering her forward. She nodded, dropping her hands and sneaking by. I closed my eyes so I couldn't follow her. So the Rogue Narrator wouldn't know where she went.

Right as she crept past Roger's door, the knob jiggled. I held my breath, not daring to reveal myself.

"Gunther? Is that you?" I kept my eyes closed, refusing to acknowledge Roger, and refusing to see where Milla went. The doorknob jiggled again. "I know it's you. Stop this childishness at once."

The jiggling became more aggressive, and I gnawed on my tongue. I sensed Milla getting situated so she wouldn't make any noises. I described it as vague as I could so the Rogue Narrator couldn't deduce where she was. Roger might be unnaturally good at hearing noises right now, just for the sake of a story.

The knob jiggled again. "Gunther! Come on!"

"It's not me. It's just stuck." I wiggled the knob. "I'm trying, but I'm not having much luck."

"What did you do?" Roger asked.

"Nothing. I swear."

"Then why don't I believe you?"

Milla was situated and holding her breath as I let go of the knob. The door flew open, whacking Roger in the face. He gave a shout of surprise before grabbing his eyebrow. "Gunther!"

"Fixed it." I tried to smile.

Roger glared at me with one eye, the other covered with his hand. "You are incorrigible."

"Thank you."

He pushed past me. "And an idiot. I thought you were supposed to be good with words."

I frowned, following behind him down the hall. "What makes you think I'd be good with words?"

He slowed his steps as he mulled over what I said, the smallest frown on his face. "I don't know. Why *would* I think you're good with words?"

His slow steps spiked my anxiety, since I wanted him out of the manor house. I linked elbows with him in the most natural way I could make it, meaning it wasn't natural at all. "To saving Veniloria!" I said, mostly to distract Roger from this awkward moment.

We walked forward at a pace I tried to make as normal as possible. Roger frowned, noticing our linked arms before looking at me again. He dropped my arm, easing me a respectful distance away from him. By that point, we were out of the house, and Roger used the opportunity to march away from me, toward the moat.

"I don't know about you, but I'm excited to get back to digging." I stretched my blistered fingers. Even though my hands looked nasty with some blisters already popped, I could pretend to be excited. I even used the right word, which meant I wasn't nearly as flustered.

Roger slowed his steps before stopping completely. He turned to stare at the manor house as he frowned and rubbed his forehead where the door hit. The imprint of where it whacked him would be red for a bit, but I doubted it would bruise. "Why do I feel like returning?"

He was about to step back toward the house, and I panicked. "We've got to get back to the moat and protect ourselves from the cursed creatures."

"Yes, I know that, but... but I still feel like I've got to go back. I must have forgotten something."

"Do you remember who created you?"

His stoic face returned as I trampled on this sensitive topic. "I remember."

"What if the evil God is trying to distract you so you aren't out there digging? Keeping you from protecting Vaywell."

It was a solid misdirect. It took some concentration to remember how to breathe. Somehow, I forgot. Breathe in, expand lungs; let the breath out... exhale the stuff in the lungs. Was I pausing enough times between my breaths? Was I getting enough oxygen in my system? Could Roger pick up the smallest irregularity of my lung capacity and know it was all a lie?

He nodded with emphasized stoicism. "You're right. I'll muscle through the emotion."

Which made me blink. With all the emotions this man was stuffing down, it would only take a small thing to make him burst.

It didn't matter. I had convinced Roger to stay away from the manor house. We walked past the archway to the moat, both taking shovels. Roger began digging, and I moved in right beside him. I tried to smile at his stoicism before forcing my broken blisters to accept their fate. I wasn't leaving Roger's side. The Rogue Narrator would not get Milla.

# Chapter Twenty

## MILLA IS SOMEWHERE

I stayed beside Roger as we focused on digging the moat. Despite his stoicism, I could tell he was distracted. It had been hours since the women and children left, but I needed to make sure no one discovered Milla until tonight. By tonight, it would be too late for someone to get on a horse and run her to the others.

It turned into mid-morning, with the promise of another hot day.

"So, Roger. Tell me about yourself," I blurted out.

He paused in his digging, then gave me a look. "Sorry?"

"We've known each other for a day or two now." Saying the time frame out loud made me realize I had been at over fifty percent for way too long. I wouldn't last another week. That much was certain. "I feel like I barely know you."

He narrowed his eyes before driving his shovel into the ground with surprising force. "You know about my wife's death."

My blisters screamed for mercy as I gathered another shovelful of dirt. I cleared my throat. "Yeah. About that, I'm... sorry. I'm really sorry she died. And that I was..."

"Insensitive?"

"Uh, yeah. Sorry. Again."

The stoicism melted away to reveal... dry. He gave me a dry look. We dug in silence. I wanted to say something more, but how could I? It was hard having a conversation with Roger when I constantly made a fool of myself in front of him.

Roger sighed, leaning against his shovel. "Can I... can I tell you something? In confidence?"

I dropped the dirt on the pile behind us. "Do you trust me to keep it from the others?" I tried to make it sound friendly enough. However, reminding him who he was talking to might make him rethink the direction of our conversation.

Roger glanced around before rubbing his forehead. "Believe me, I don't want to tell you. But this has been annoying me, and maybe if I get it off my chest, I'll be able to focus. See, my wife and I were... we were done with our marriage."

The shovel blade buried deeper into the ground. I used it to lean against, light enough to not topple into the moat. I tried not to let any surprise show on my face. "You were done?"

He wiped the sweat from his forehead. "We were great friends, but we both knew soon after our marriage it wouldn't work."

Unease trickled out of my soul and into my facial expressions. I didn't have Roger's stoicism. No one knew about my ex-wife. Maybe Tara did, but she never brought it up again. I made certain no one in my story understood what divorce meant, since it was still a tender subject for me.

"If there was a way to legally end our marriage, we would have." Roger talked as though reading my thoughts. "Gone our separate ways. Made a life both of us would've actually enjoyed."

Oof, that was a blow. The Rogue Narrator knew I was divorced, so he created a character that wanted the thing that caused me so much pain. My eye twitched, but I did my best not to react.

It was then that Roger's eyes flitted to the manor house. The Rogue Narrator let me sense the scene from the night before playing in his character's mind. The way Paldric made out with Tara. Roger's stoic face was in place because he refused to make a reaction, even though the desire was there. My jaw dropped open.

Oh no. No, no, no. The threat's still there.

**"Don't you dare obsess about it again. Don't. You. Dare,"** Devin said.

Why was he explaining this to me? He had to know it made me feel like he was evil.

"I know this probably makes you think I'm evil." He was literally saying my thoughts out loud. This had to be a move by the Rogue Narrator. Devin? Is the code there?

**"No, it's not. But the Rogue Narrator is unusually persuasive in what Roger is saying right now."**

"But... but it's been troubling me for a year. I know how it makes me look. I know, by saying it to you, that you will assume I planned it all out in order to murder her."

I had little to say, because—yes. Yes, I did think that, but only for a moment. Roger looked distressed, and confirming to him how I still believed he possessed an evil streak wouldn't help.

"But I would never murder my wife. I loved her, but as a dear friend. She and I cared about each other, but we shouldn't have married. I swear to you, I did not murder her."

My fingers curled around the shovel handle as I pulled it out of the dirt. I straightened my glasses before focusing on my work. "Why are you telling me this?"

Roger covered his face and let out a groan. "I don't know. I honestly, truly, do not know. This entire thing is making me uncomfortable, and I'm—" he dropped his hands and picked up his shovel again. "I'm sorry. When I saw Tara for the first time, it was almost like hope returned for—" A noise escaped my throat, one that shouldn't have been loud, but it cut Roger off with my unintelligible sputtering. My shovel slipped into the moat. Roger looked at the shovel in the hole, then at me. "Are you alright?"

My blistered hands were in my hair. "Perfectly fine." I jumped into the hole to retrieve the shovel. "So, it must have hurt you far more than you let on when you saw Paldric making out with Tara."

Yes, it was harsh. Yes, I was once again making myself out to be the insensitive jerk by rubbing this in his face, but I tried to sound as detached as possible.

**"Oh, Gunther. You're getting obsessed again,"** Devin mumbled.

He practically admitted he still had feelings, and I needed to remind him what happened at the ball. Roger is a nobleman. He wouldn't dare try to break them up for his own gain. Tara wouldn't like that.

I glanced back at Roger. He clammed up, the stoic look returning to his face as he got busy with his work. Yep. Sometimes I really am a jerk, aren't I.

**"Yes."**

Doesn't matter. I still cannot trust Roger right now. He needs to stay away from Tara. She wouldn't like it if Roger forced her and Paldric to break up.

I said it in my mind with such confidence that Tara's character file opened, and this fresh addition dropped in.

Ha! There. Now it's in her code. It must have sensed my narrator voice, even though I spoke it in my head. It would have been worse to say that sentence out loud.

**"Speaking of code, Roger is overwhelmed with a strong desire to return to the manor. The Rogue Narrator is hitting him with everything he's got. He wants to find Milla, and it's getting harder for Roger to ignore it."**

I didn't know what to do, so I scraped my shovel against the side of the moat to make it bigger. "Don't worry about it, Roger. I mean, the Dark Wizard will arrive in a couple of days. It's enough for anyone to—"

Roger, collapsing to his knees above me, cut my little speech off. My eyes widened as I watched the guy fall forward, all the color leaving his face. I dropped my shovel and grabbed him before he fell into the partial moat and snapped his neck. A few other filler characters helped me drag him back up, placing him on his back. I climbed out of the hole, worried.

Paldric ran forward, dropping to his knees next to me. "Is he alright? What happened?"

"The heat of the day is getting to him," one of my filler characters said.

"It's still early morning." I didn't mean for it to sound like a challenge.

"A lot of us suffered with it yesterday," the character said.

"Get the man some water!" someone else shouted.

Roger cracked his eyes open, blinking a few times. "Forgive me." He groaned, trying to get up. "Forgive me, all. The stress has affected my ability to work this morning."

"Get some rest, Roger. We'll be just fine. We need you in good health for the battle ahead," Paldric said.

He nodded as Paldric helped him to his feet. "I guess I will return to the manor house after all."

I sucked in a breath, then grabbed his arm, moving it around my shoulder. "I'll help you get there."

"Gunther, it's—"

"No trouble at all," I filled in for Paldric. "It really isn't. I'll make sure he's settled before I come back."

Roger just looked confused as I propelled us toward the manor house.

"Make sure Tara checks in on him. She can help," Paldric said.

I kept walking, glaring at the manor house in the distance. "Yep. Of course. Absolutely. She'll be there."

Paldric frowned but couldn't say much else because we were already moving past him.

# Chapter Twenty-One

# I Make a Threat

We passed the gate and headed straight for the manor house when Roger finally spoke. "You don't want me and Tara together." I said nothing as we kept walking. He resisted, yanking my arm away from his shoulders as we both came to a stop. "Gunther, I commend your ability to fake your concern, but I can return to the manor house on my own."

"Nonsense, you might have another episode. It's only getting hotter, and I've got to make sure you rest."

"With Tara watching out for me?" Roger asked.

"Well, you know, with... with someone."

His glare darkened. "I never should have told you. I knew it was a mistake."

"You told me because the evil God forced you to tell me. To remind me you are..." I trailed off, at least having the self-control for that.

"That I'm still a threat?" Roger filled in for me. I said nothing, because I learned my lesson about revealing too much, but it backfired on me. "I swear to you I never murdered my wife. And I swear to you, I would never murder my friends. That is not who I am. There is nothing the evil God can do to convince me."

I didn't like this conversation, but it needed to happen. Roger needed to understand. "You don't know the power he has. There is little I can do if he comes for you, and you cannot stop the code once it appears. I'm sorry, Roger. I truly am. But you're still a threat."

He shook his head, brushing me off. My mind clawed for some plan as we got closer to the front door of the manor house. Roger sighed and slowed to a stop, causing me to stop as well. He turned his head, but his back was still facing me. "You've gone out of your way to make sure I'm not welcome here ever since we met." Roger seemed to freeze, then turned completely. "So, why have you been helping me all morning?"

The Rogue Narrator knew Milla was still here, and I bet he would give Roger every bit of help to make a logical leap.

I approached him. "It's hot for morning time, and you've been stressing for most of it."

Roger turned to look at me, a frown evident on his face. "Are you... are you hiding something?"

My heart rate spiked, but my voice remained steady. "You never got water when you passed out before. It would be a pity if you dropped again."

Right as I said it, Roger groaned, his eyes rolling back again. His knees gave out, and I grabbed him to catch his fall.

**"Whoa, whoa. What was that?"** Devin asked.

Nothing.

**"Did you use your powers?"**

Of course not.

Tara burst out of the manor, holding her skirts to help her run straight for me. "What have you done? Why is your percentage being odd again?"

**"Gunther!"**

"I don't know what happened." I said it to Devin and Tara, even if it was a lie for both of them.

**"I read that. You can't hide it."**

Devin wasn't amused.

**"Of course I'm not amused! You woke up with a spike in percentage! The Dark Wizard is still a couple days away, and you *cannot* last if this continues!"**

I eased Roger to the ground as Tara grabbed his other arm to help me. "What's going on? Why is my percentage weird?"

"It's like it was when Roger threatened you. The percentage was… I don't know how to explain it. It's getting ready to rise, even though it hasn't yet," Tara said.

I nodded, relieved.

**"Nope! Don't you dare relax. You still have me to answer to. I don't like how this day is playing out. This is textbook definition of an unreliable narrator, and I cannot, as a Guardian, let this continue."**

Tara ordered me to get some water, so I went inside, planning to help Devin understand.

I don't know what this morning was about. I honestly don't. Whatever happened between last night and this morning, it's completely gone from my memory. And yeah, it terrifies me. Eventually I will get that mental puzzle organized and put together, but right now I'm worried about Milla. The Rogue Narrator is doing everything he can to isolate my little girl character, and I can't let him.

**"This is bad. I can't stress that enough."** I grabbed a pitcher and filled a cup with water. **"You are dangerously high with your percentage. You're acting far more unstable, and we're only halfway through your story."**

The cup got about half full when I paused, glancing at the ceiling, surprised and relieved. Halfway? Really? That's great news.

**"Alright, I'm going to need you to think cynically right now. You are convincing yourself to stay even though you used far too much of your powers. It's a little more than halfway, and you know Roger isn't nearly as deadly as you originally thought. Yes, this has forced me to break a promise, but I must ask you to consider leaving your book."**

I took the cup, heading back outside. The morning was comfortably warm, and when I saw Roger struggling to sit up, with Tara's arms around him like that, I picked up the pace.

**"Gunther, focus. We're having a conversation right now."**

I'm not leaving, Devin. Can't and won't. Not until I know more about the Rogue Narrator's secret code in Roger.

**"Is it worth your sanity? Is it worth the thought of destroying them? You've got to get out."**

Roger took the glass from me, and Tara instructed him to take it in sips. He obeyed, his eyes lingering on her face far too much for my liking.

"Come on, let's get you in a bed. Just you. In a bed. A room, really. Perhaps on the ground," I said like an idiot.

Tara stood, frowning. "Gunther—" An entire slew of information about healing came to me as I looked at Tara. If we moved him too soon, it might make him pass out again. He was in danger of heat stroke and needed rest.

"We've got to get him in a cooler place. It's getting hot out here," I said instead.

Roger nodded, and once again I helped him to his feet before Tara took over, leading him toward the door. Roger rested his hand on her shoulder as she wrapped her arm around his waist. He then glanced at me with his stupid, impossible to read face. I glared, watching them make their slow way to the manor house.

**"Don't tempt this. Don't press your luck. Please get out."**

I moved forward and watched as Roger kept rubbing his head, looking like he was ready to succumb to a panic attack.

**"He will. According to his code, the Rogue Narrator is pressuring him to search every inch of the manor house for something he feels he forgot. The important thing he forgot is the only thing that will clear his mind."**

The three of us walked down the hallway of the manor house, me at a respectable distance, though Roger kept glancing behind his shoulder. I smiled back, because I didn't know what else to do. I let them enter a guest room, waiting by the wall.

This is a message for the Rogue Narrator, currently infiltrating my book and trying to drive me insane.

**"Gunther,"** Devin warned.

I don't know who you are, but you're clearly trying to get Roger to find Milla. Find her so you can get me. Roger, in his own way, convinced you to change your mind last night, so let me try now. I am halfway done with my story, and I have no intention of leaving.

**"Gun—"**

Jim made it so there's only seventy thousand words, which means you've got less than thirty-five thousand to find and break me. The Dark Wizard won't be here for another day or two, at least. And I've just spent who knows how long this morning chasing Roger around, locking him in his room, convincing him to faint. The man is suffering, and I will continue to let him suffer, because it's padding my word count. You keep trying to find her, and I'll keep stopping him. Maybe I'll make more elaborate ways to keep bloating that word count until the story is done, and I leave. Or nothing at all can happen for the next few days and the device summarizes everything in a time jump. I'll even let it jump to when the Dark Wizard brings his army, and the battle happens. Would you like to face me in battle? Or should I find more ways to lock Roger away?

**"This is extremely dangerous. You cannot stay in your story for that long. Not at over fifty percent. You have a death wish for your characters."**

I leave it in your hands, Rogue Narrator.

There was a beat of silence as I waited for what I expected to hear.

"I'm alright, Tara. Better than alright, actually. I—" Roger sighed. "I feel a lot better. You really are a skilled healer. I should get back out there. We don't know when the Dark Wizard will arrive."

I smirked.

**"Gunther,"** Devin whispered.

Time jump it is, then. See you on the battlefield, Rogue.

# Chapter Twenty-Two

# TIME JUMPS AND FLASHBACKS

Alright, I'll admit it first. It felt awesome threatening the Rogue Narrator like that. But here I was, two and a half days later, standing between Paldric and Alwin with my arms folded, trying to keep the terror from my face. With the roaring trolls and the goblins going berserk in the sunlight, I doubted my internal monologue sounded nearly as cool. So, I'm going to remember that once I was intimidating, instead of focusing on the way my knees quaked under me.

**"Oh, nice, the written part of the screen is finally picking up the words. It must have taken your threat seriously about not documenting anything for two days,"** Jim said.

I bet the Rogue Narrator is happy about that.

**"Yeah, um, please don't antagonize the Rogue Narrator again,"** Jim said.

Jim was here, of course. It was getting toward dinner time in the real world, even though it was late afternoon here. Devin not only needed a break, but also sleep.

**"You have a nasty battle ahead, that's for sure."**

But you know what? I also promised the device would summarize everything leading up to this point. I never specified how long that would be. So, let's summarize what happened the past two days, and pray to the God of this story—me—that it'll translate to a ton of words. Because that would be great. Fine, even. Spectacular. Picturesque. Amazing. Breathtaking.

Jim snorted. **"I hope you're better at describing your past instead of regurgitating a thesaurus."**

I'm trying my best, Jim. Those cursed creatures are terrifying. Petrifying. Horrifying.

**"Are you good with flowery descriptions of the past, Gunther?"**

Uh, no. No, not really.

**"Alright. Well, summarize away. Take your time. Those trolls look ready to eat someone."**

Hey, I had that experience once. Onward to the past! But not so far into the past that we go back to that time where a troll gnawed on my face because I had the pleasure of that experience back in book one. No, we'll just jump back to the past couple of days.

Milla climbed out of her hiding spot soon after dinner, when we had almost finished the delectable meat pie. Paldric asked Tara if she wanted the last slice when Milla peeked over the wall, staring at the pie with wide, hungry eyes since she ate no lunch. There were ten seconds of pure silence as we all stared at each other before the arguments began. While the arguments happened, I passed the remaining piece of pie toward Milla, and she dug into it voraciously. With an unquenchable appetite. Uncontrolled need to fill her stomach. Padding her empty stomach like I'm trying to pad the word count.

They all started bickering about what was best, and I eased myself into the conversation to make sure they understood it was too late to send her away. Which caused Roger to glare at me, and I realized my actions caused his stuffed down dam of emotions to explode, destroying his stoicism. With a face full of anger, he accused me of doing this somehow. Milla, being a child and prone to always telling the truth, confirmed Roger's suspicions. She then elaborated how I ushered her past the door I was holding close, and how she heard him jostling the knob and trying to get out. I sat there, a hand to my mouth, simply bracing for the blowup.

Needless to say, it didn't make me popular with the adults in the room. Roger, Alwin, Paldric, and Tara took turns lecturing me about how incredibly dangerous Vaywell would be, and how it was no place for a child. Well, Alwin and Paldric were lecturing as calmly as they could. Tara's tone was a lot sharper. Roger shouted at me the entire time. That man was angry. Exasperated. Irate. And he showed it.

**"Did you study a thesaurus before this?"**

This was the last straw for Roger, and I took his shouting. Which meant I said nothing as he screamed how he wished he could have a battle of wits with me, but his noble upbringing made it impossible to fight an unarmed man. Poetic, really. He realized why he felt the need to check the manor house, and once he spent his anger, he stormed out of the room. Devin reported he went into a depressive funk about it all. Which I was sort of responsible for. Okay, I was one hundred percent responsible.

Later that evening, he and I talked, and he admitted he was wrong to blow up at me. However, he couldn't watch another person he cared about be threatened by the cursed creatures. Especially a defenseless little girl. It hurt him too much and brought back nasty memories of his wife's death. I admitted knowing why the Rogue Narrator pressured him so hard. If the evil God tried to get Milla to leave with the women and children, then it was proof he wanted to kidnap her to draw us all out. Roger felt better about Milla staying, but only a little. Both of us knew it was still perilous for her here, but Lord Adrijian assured us she would not step one foot on the battlefield. If the evil army somehow broke through our defenses, every person in the manor would protect her with their lives.

**"Great, Gunther. You're doing great. This is logging into the device, and the word count is climbing. Keep going."**

Well, I mean, I can't think of much else. The Rogue Narrator was true to his promise. Nothing much happened the next two days except for preparations. We spent all day digging the moat and barely got it finished, with a layer of water covering the spikes. Something told me it would kill a ton of goblins when they started running toward us. Until their dead bodies would fill the moat and the others would just walk over them.

I screwed up my face in disgust at the thought. It was gross, and also exactly what these goblins would do.

**"Is that all you're going to say about the past two days?"** Jim asked.

Well, I mean, if you have any other ideas to pad the word count, I'm all—

Oh! I remember! There was that time Roger caught Paldric and Tara making out in Paldric's room!

Oops, spoiled it a bit, but let's keep going. That was a brilliant scene. I was at first proud of remembering another scene, but then deflated at the memory. I knew Roger well enough by now that I recognized the surprise and pain on his stoic face when he opened a door and stumbled into that. It was partially my fault again. Honestly, Roger had every right to hate me. I've been a jerk to him.

But yeah. I was hanging around the hallway, letting Paldric and Tara have their moment. It was actually a great character-building scene, and I felt annoyed, vexed, and antagonized when Devin said the device didn't record it. I'll have to remember it as best I can. I've done flashbacks before. That'll be a great way to add more words.

Jim? Is it working? Are we getting a flashback?

**"I see nothing yet, but focus more on how much it developed Paldric and Tara's character. Then it might…"**

I closed one eye, remembering how satisfying it was for the two of them to have this moment.

**"Yep, here we go. It's working."**

It was toward the evening of the second day. Tensions were high because the scouts reported the army would be here by tomorrow (which was now, as I watched them arrive, but this is a flashback, so they just heard the news).

**"I know how flashbacks work,"** Jim said.

It's my first time doing a flashback while in the device. Oh, except that one time in book one, but that was sort of misleading.

**"Misleading as in it was a memory you completely fabricated?"**

Hey, I've got to put a few nibbles for people who didn't read book one and went straight for the sequel.

**"This isn't getting published, and even if it is, don't you think the reader will get confused before this and give up?"**

I won't insult the intelligence of a reader who reads my stuff, Jim. It's not good business practice.

Jim laughed again before we returned to the flashback.

Paldric held his spoon weirdly at dinner so it wouldn't touch a nasty blister, and Tara noticed. I played on that because I sensed the deep concern there. And with the war looming over their heads, they were ripe to do something they wouldn't have otherwise done.

**"Not everyone craves sex the moment things get scary,"** Jim said.

No, Paldric would never do that without marrying her first. And Tara wouldn't either, after what happened... before.

So, I crept down the hall to make sure things went how I predicted and heard them talking in his room. I closed my eyes because it was easier to visualize what was happening.

Tara waited by the door. Ever since they met two weeks ago, she always felt comfortable in his room, but—

—Hold up. I understand this might mess with the flashback, but... two weeks? That's it?! That's not nearly enough time to fully flesh out a plausible romantic—

You know what? Never mind. I'm describing what happened. Things needed to be sped up in their relationship because of Roger, so let's get back to it.

It was the first time in his room since their make-out session at the ball. The atmosphere was different between them in the best way possible. Neither one wanted to breech the subject, though, but her being there added a spark.

"I was wondering if you needed any help with your hand." She held up her pack of ointments and lotions. "I saw you holding your spoon strange at dinner."

Paldric had been pacing the entire length of the room when she entered, and only stopped when she asked about his hand. He looked down at his palm. "I... yes. I seemed to have formed a blister." He held it up to show a makeshift bandage.

Tara moved farther into the room, taking his hand with one of her own. "I can check it if you'd like."

He smiled. "I'd like that very much." Tara looked around for somewhere to place her bag, but Paldric's room didn't have a small table. "You can set it on the bed if you'd like." Paldric said it without thinking until halfway through when he mentioned 'bed' in her presence. And then he wished he hadn't, and his speech slowed enough for Tara to pick up on his embarrassment. "Only if you'd like." He did not look at her.

"No, it's fine." She smiled at his awkwardness and tried not to bring attention to her own thoughts about the arrangement. They walked over to the bed, and she set her pack down before sitting on the edge. He sat next to her, holding out his hand. Her fingers worked quickly through the knot. He scooted closer to her because he wanted to make sure she got a good look at it, but he didn't mind the double bonus of being closer to her. She unwrapped it, trying not to touch his blistered hand even though Paldric wouldn't have minded.

Tara rifled through her bag of ointments before picking one out, uncorking it. "This should help the blister turn into a callous quicker."

"Thank you, Tara." He hesitated just enough before saying her name.

She pointed her smile at her lap. They were quiet as she worked, putting lotion on her hand before stroking it into his blister. It had a cooling effect to it, and Paldric appreciated the numbing agent it had. The art of healing was the only magic left in this world. Information passed down every generation to know what herbs to get. Especially ones touched by enough moonlight, where everyone assumed the elves had gone.

The last knot was done, and Tara smiled at him as she let go. "It should look better tomorrow morning, but still be careful with it."

His fingers traced over the bandage. "The moat is practically done. A few men will be out there with shovels to make sure the ocean water gets in, and then we'll be ready for them."

There was another silence, this one more uncomfortable. They successfully ignored the looming doom hanging over them for about half a minute, but now it came crashing down.

Tara placed the ointment back in her pack before setting it on her lap, and Paldric continued to play with the tied end of the bandage.

"Just... um..." she tried not to let her true feelings out. Tried not to hint how frightened she was for Paldric's safety. But tomorrow was uncertain, and it was driving her mad. "Be careful. With your bandage. In... in the battle."

"Yeah, I will."

She stood up, straightening her skirts, trying to smile. "The ointment isn't hard to make, but it's something I'd rather not do if I can help it. So... so keep your hand safe. And the rest of you, too."

"I will."

She fiddled with the edges of her pack. "Because I don't want you to get hurt."

"Gunther assured me he has a plan. He'll do everything he can to keep us safe."

"That's what I'm worried about." Her hand trembled as she tucked some hair behind her ear. She had every right to not trust me, and I wanted to be annoyed, but I couldn't. I wasn't certain about my plan, either, but I didn't need anyone else to know that.

But I said that part in my mind, which began a heated discussion between me and Devin, where I almost turned him off to keep focusing on Paldric and Tara's moment. We'll ignore Devin's mistrust for now to keep the flow of the flashback.

Paldric touched her shoulder, smiling, letting his optimism shine through. "I fully trust you to stop him before he hurts anyone."

"I can't if I'm here at the manor house and you and him are on the same battlefield," Tara said.

Paldric smiled. "At least Milla will be safe."

"And I will do everything in my power to keep her that way."

Paldric still smiled, because he was the kind of person who always found a reason for optimism. Tara tried to match his smile, but it failed. Instead, she kissed him, which he liked a lot better. I leaned against the wall with my eyes closed so I wouldn't disturb them. Tara grabbed fistfuls of Paldric's shirt, forcing him near her as he wrapped his arms firmly around her, making sure she wasn't going anywhere. Their lips did not bother starting out gently. They already finished the gentleness with the bandaging. A battle was looming, and they needed to make the most of their moments alone. It was extremely difficult to describe what they were doing while I was simultaneously easing Devin's concern about how I was a reliable narrator. Tara and Paldric probably appreciated some privacy, as I gave Devin my conclusive arguments as to why he could trust my plan.

**"Most of his distrust stems from you never telling him the plan in the first place,"** Jim said.

Hey, it's too confusing for you to comment about a conversation I'm only summarizing while in a flashback.

**"Yeah, alright. Devin's still convinced you're hiding something."**

And we return to the flashback, where I stayed as quiet as I could since I've heard I ruin romantic moments.

Somewhere, Jim snorted, but I refuse to comment on it to not break the immersion of the flashback again.

Which is when I heard Roger walk by. I barely had time to open my eyes when he gave me a curt nod in greeting as he opened the door. "Hey, Paldric, I wanted to—" He stopped short, raising an eyebrow as Paldric and Tara broke apart, looking at him with redder cheeks. Roger cleared his throat. "Forgive me. I'll ask later." He closed the door, his hand remaining on the knob. It didn't take Tara and Paldric too long before they were lip locked again. But Roger stared at the opposite wall before glancing in my direction. I tried to smile, but this entire set up made me seem like a peeper.

Roger narrowed his eyes before releasing his hand on the knob. I didn't need Devin to tell me his thoughts. Roger could have been lying about his love for Tara, but I saw it that night. Saw the ache, the pain, the way he tried so desperately to rein it in because there was someone else watching him. He gave me a smile that never touched his eyes before disappearing down the hall.

And yeah, I felt bad for the guy. If I was being honest, he was the most complex character in this story, and I would tip my hat to the Rogue Narrator for creating such an interesting character. Someone with evil intentions created Roger, yet he himself was good, and that was fascinating. His life wasn't completely evil, and it was enough for me to feel sorry for him.

Which is what the Rogue Narrator probably wanted.

**"I'm rooting for him to be good. And you wrote an entire chapter with a flashback. Nice,"** Jim said.

Oh, really? Perfect. The Rogue Narrator's going to hate that.

**"Well, I mean, it's odd that the cursed creatures let you have that. This might be part of the Rogue Narrator's plan,"** Jim said.

No doubt. But I will take every opportunity.

# Chapter Twenty-Three

# Spoiler Alert: The Cursed Creatures Don't Let Me Finish

**"Oh, I got a text from Devin. Give me a sec to read it."**

I waited, awkwardly, as a group of trolls below started stomping on the ground, roaring. It was unsettling, and Alwin tightened his grip over the glowing sword.

**"He says you're being unreliable again. You haven't said everything that happened these past two days."**

Well, as much as I'd love to go over every detail of the past two days, I don't remember much else of significance the device would record. Milla figuring out a way to stay and my two love birds making out were the big memories. Everything else was boring preparation for this tense battle right now. I could try to conjure up some details about how ridiculously hot it was the past few days while digging that moat, but... yeah. There you go. It was boiling.

**"Apparently, you and Devin had a lot of talks over the past two days about your memory. Not just the conversation while Paldric and Tara were kissing."**

Oh, yeah, that's right! I forgot that too.

**"He said this doesn't help his opinion of you. He's still convinced you're hiding something from us."**

Tell Devin he's being unreliable now too, since he's supposed to be asleep. Is he hiding the fact that he's tracking my story right now?

**"He's following along on his work laptop that is most likely at his home. And he's texting me again. I'll let you know when it comes through."**

I will admit I'm not a war writer. Sure, my characters fought off a dragon in my original draft, but wars were not something I was prepared to write. Yesterday Lord Adrijian asked if I wanted to take over the command, and I said absolutely not, because I didn't know what I was doing. Which, in hindsight, wasn't the best thing to admit out loud to a large group of people when some of them knew I was the God of this realm. I didn't exactly bolster anyone's faith in that meeting.

**"Devin is still waiting for you to recap what you two talked about."**

Considering there was an army of goblins and trolls out there, my sigh didn't sound too weird, but Alwin gave me a strange look.

Devin and I have been trying to figure out why I couldn't remember anything two mornings ago. Two? Three? When *was* that?

**"Uh... back in chapter eighteen."**

Fair enough. Devin and I have been trying to piece together what happened, but he is now convinced I know something more. The guy is stubborn and won't trust me at all.

**"Because you keep brushing it aside."**

Devin? Is that you? Aren't you supposed to be asleep?

**"I commend you for remaining at fifty-seven percent for two days, but I cannot let this go. We need to figure out why your percentage jumped if we're going to get it down,"** Devin said.

Which I completely understand. Once I finish this battle, I'll be out of my story, so it won't matter, anyway.

**"You think you can write a twenty-five thousand word battle sequence when you yourself admitted to never writing a war scene before? Or are you promis-**

**ing you will leave after the battle, no matter how many words are left?"** Devin asked.

I gnawed on the inside of my cheek, closing one eye as I saw a nasty troll give another roar. The goblins took that as a sign and started running straight for us. Paldric tightened his grip on his sword, and Alwin shouted a command. A hundred arrows shot over our heads, raining down on the enemy. Tension was high, the archers were already getting their arrows ready for another wave, and the catapult was waiting for Alwin's signal.

And yes, I need to break away from the action to mention *another* thing I forgot.

**"I see why you're not good with war scenes,"** Devin mumbled.

Ouch, Devin. At least it's not getting published.

So, anyway, Alwin revealed his elf-ness back at the party, which tripled his popularity overnight. He's spent the days making sure everyone knew he didn't want to rule the humans, and he wanted to lie low. But no one, not even the secret narrator of a story, could deny everyone was in awe of him.

Alwin sheathed the sword in the current time and pulled out a bow, notching the arrow almost as fast as he released it. The arrow sailed into the air before burying into the troll's eye. I raised an eyebrow, impressed. The troll barely had time to gasp before dropping on about five goblins.

And this, dear reader, who is not actually reading this because it's not published, is a simple example of show don't tell. See, I shouldn't have broken away from the action to tell you pointless information when I could have simply described the looks of awe on the men's face when they watched Alwin showing off his awesome elf self.

Elf self, that's fun to say.

Alwin almost lowered his bow before bringing it up again, shooting another arrow that took down one more troll. The men next to him watched, their eyes already wide and their jaws slack. I doubted they could get more shocked. Humans passed the myths and legends of the elves down, but it was completely different to see it play before their eyes. On the battlefield, two dead trolls were on their backs with arrows sticking out of their eyes, far from the moat. Alwin shouted for the catapults, and the very rocks flew at his command.

"Focus, men." Alwin pulled out his glowing sword again. "They will not stop until we're dead. And I don't want you to die."

The men nodded, returning their attention to the battle ahead. They faced an army of cursed creatures, and yet heard the thing so many of them grew up fearing. That elves didn't think they were worth saving and left them to the fate of the Dark Wizard. Some of them were nervous about Alwin. After a century, many of the people didn't think highly of elves, but a bigger enemy was after them. Everyone wanted to put aside their prejudice to take care of the cursed creatures.

Goblins filled the moat at an alarming rate. It took two days for us to dig that thing. Seeing it used up in the first fifteen minutes of the war made me reconsider whether I could push this battle to twenty-five thousand words. I had a goal to stretch this out to at least ten thousand, but that moat filled up fast.

Ugh, I didn't know how I was going to survive this.

**"And you'd survive better if you were being completely honest with everyone."**

Good thing I am, Devin.

He groaned. **"Good night, Gunther."**

Sleep well.

In their frenzied state, the goblins did not bother waiting for the moat to fill with the dead bodies of their brothers. They entered the ocean to go around the moat, which filled me with relief. Good thing I planned for that.

Devin came back with a vengeance. **"When? When did you plan for that?"**

That man wouldn't get any sleep at this rate.

**"Answer the question."**

While eating dinner, when everyone else went over the war plan, I made plans of my own. The second the goblin bodies touched the ocean, it awakened the Siludontia, who came fast. I had placed a strong desire for goblin meat in the Siludontia's character, and it caused him to head straight for the beach. Oh, hey! Is this the first time I mention the Siludontia by name in the sequel?

**"Yes. All the other times you just mention a shark,"** Jim said.

Alright! Let's stretch this out!

The beach was shallow as the goblins stepped into it. Their filth, their essence, trickled through the water, awakening him at once. Since yours truly blinded him back in book one, he became reliant on his other senses, and lucky for him, goblins reeked. He swam, the dorsal fin sticking out of the ocean, the desire to eat those goblins driving him to do things he wouldn't otherwise try. One of them even got a cut on their leg, and the dark purple blood created a frenzy in the shark.

The goblins were at the shallow end, fighting with some men, who were instructed to stay out of the water. Despite the frenzy, the Siludontia was still a smart creature. He leapt out of the water, revealing himself with his five eyes and well over a hundred teeth gleaming in the late afternoon sun. One look at this threat in the sunlight, and the goblins whipped themselves into a fury. Despite the school-bus sized shark with gorged out eyes in the deeper end of the shallows, the goblins ran straight for it, because it was the bigger threat. The men could wait. The five eyed, multilayered teeth creature needed to be taken care of right now. And they needed to run right into the creature's habitat to get it.

I watched, proud, as a good chunk of the goblin army broke off to fight the Siludontia. Watched as the shark lured them into the deeper end and chomped at them, churning up the water full of purple goblin blood. It brought smaller sharks to come snack on the remains as they dropped into the ocean. The Siludontia alone, just as I had planned, would cut the goblin army in half. Yes, that shark terrified me, but that thing was mine, and I would use him well.

**"Nice,"** Jim said.

I unsheathed my sword, knowing I wasn't nearly as well trained. I could play with book logic and have Alwin train me for two days before suddenly becoming better, but I doubted it would work. Not without pushing my God powers.

**"Yeah, not a smart idea. Best to do what you can with what you have,"** Jim said.

I'd hate to interrupt Devin's sleep again.

**"Oh, what's the point? I'll see how much I can monitor before I doze off,"** Devin said.

**"In the middle of a battle sequence?"** Jim asked.

**"Leave my poor old sleeping habits alone."**

The first of the goblins traveled over their dead brothers, and I let out a nervous breath, trying to concentrate. I convinced myself to not use powers that might cause a percentage, but this was a battle that threatened the lives of my characters. The temptation would be strong.

# Chapter Twenty-Four

## THE BATTLE

The archers hit the goblins and trolls again, mostly goblins dropping dead as the trolls collected arrows on their bodies. Alwin tried again to hit one of them in the eye, but with the battle becoming more chaotic, he couldn't get a clear shot.

Alwin drove forward with his band of men, holding the glowing sword and shield aloft as—

Paldric shouted as a goblin tried to stab him, but he barely got out of the—

The men following Alwin hacked away at the goblins, bodies crunching together in a—

A goblin was after me, terrifying me as I tried to stab it with my—

Paldric stabbed a goblin through the heart, not noticing he was pulled away from his—

And then I realized why it was so hard to write battle scenes. Usually, narrators had it well planned out, every kernel of action stacked up in a perfect mosaic of chaos. I had planned none of this. Not the action, anyway. I was describing this spur of the moment, and I couldn't keep up. I had to ignore a group in order to focus on the one.

Paldric tried to keep himself from getting surrounded or to not panic as the goblins drew around him. I did my best getting to my main character, making sure he knew he wasn't alone as chaos continued to distract me.

Roger was somewhere. I couldn't sense him. The battle grew, and the men pushed back.

I broke through the circle of goblins. In the time it took me to stab a goblin through the heart, Paldric already cut down three.

"You're fantastic at this," I said.

He finished stabbing another goblin, taking a quick breather. "I hate to tell you this, but I only look good because you're... not."

Yeah, I deserved that. "Let's just say sword fighting is not popular where I'm from."

"That brings me comfort to know heaven isn't full of battles with goblins."

A noise escaped me as I thought about all the brutal and bloody wars in my history's past, and dropped the conversation. It was easy, what with goblins trying to hack at us.

We worked on the circle of goblins, and I managed to not reveal how invincible I was, which was fine by me. The Rogue Narrator knew, but if he'd somehow point me out to these cursed creatures then—

You know what? I've given the guy enough ideas for now. Let's just leave that thought unfinished.

The trolls came. They may have better mental control in the sunlight, but they were still stupid. A ten-foot-tall troll swung his club thingy, not caring if he hit goblins or men.

**"I believe that's a cudgel, if you don't want to keep calling it a club thingy,"** Jim said.

Ah, yes. Cudgel. Fun word to say.

If it irked the goblins that trolls kept missing men and hitting them, they didn't show it. In fact, it was terrifying how undeterred the goblins looked about getting trampled or hit by their fellow creatures. The goblins surged after the men, screaming and howling as they hacked at them, ignoring the trolls. I even watched as a goblin got hit with the cudgel and still tried to stab a man in the legs before finally dying. I couldn't tell if they felt exhaustion. They just ran after us in a rage. The Dark Wizard had goblins to burn, apparently.

After hacking another goblin to the ground, I wondered why. Why didn't the Dark Wizard wait in the shadows for the sun to set? I glanced at the chaos, and despite how hopeless I felt at the beginning, we were winning. The ocean was now an all-you-could-eat buffet for the sea creatures. The trolls were a beast to fight, yes, but they were killing more goblins than men. There were at least two hundred shadow soldiers, but it was late afternoon. Why didn't the Dark Wizard just wait a few more hours to send his entire army?

And then I realized I didn't know where Roger was, which spiked my already rocketing heart rate. Jim? Devin? Can you track him for me?

**"Over by Alwin,"** Jim said.

The action moved too fast. Paldric already moved on to the next group as I caught my breath, sensing Alwin and his group of men taking on two trolls at a time. Roger must be among them. I shook out my right hand as I moved. My blisters made themselves known, and a small part of my brain ordered me to heal them, but I ignored the nagging.

I ran, and some goblins noticed me, but I wasn't a big enough threat yet for them to break away from their battles. I caught up with Alwin and his men.

My elf was doing the thing that was becoming his signature move. He stood on the shoulders of the troll before shoving an arrow straight into his eye. I winced in sympathy, because that could not be a comfortable way to die. The other men hacked at the second troll, bringing the creature to its knees before slicing its throat. Another unpleasant way to go, if I really wanted to think about it, but I had no time.

Alwin leapt to the ground, falling lightly to his feet before straightening as I ran up to him. "Have you seen Roger?" My elf glanced around, then pointed to a recognizable figure not that far. I patted Alwin on the back. "Thank you."

The men moved to the next group of trolls. My elf felt anxious, because he wanted to be among the trees. He'd have a better vantage point to surprise the trolls, but there weren't any trees nearby. None of us dared go into territory where the shadow soldiers lurked. Unless it was on accident, like how Roger stood dangerously close as he fought off a troll.

I strode forward, feeling sick to my stomach. Roger stepped back, his legs brushing up against the shadow leaves. Black fingers stretched for his pant leg, trying to grasp the material.

"Roger!" I slammed my sword against the fingers. The blackness retreated with a hiss.

He finished slicing the troll's belly before he turned and noticed me stabbing the shadows and backed away, taking a few deep breaths. "What? What was that?"

"Stay away from the shadows," I said.

He frowned as the troll he sliced dropped dead. Roger stared at the woods he accidentally got too close to. His eyes widened as he took another step back. I plainly saw how terrified he was at the prospect of the Dark Wizard capturing him.

I patted his back. "You're alright now."

Roger shot a glance over his shoulder before pushing me out of the way and leaping in time to miss a cudgel hitting the ground with a dull thud. It would have killed us both if it wasn't for his fast thinking.

No, wait. It would have killed Roger. I would have been just—

**"Try not to think about it,"** Devin said.

Right, ignoring my invulnerability.

The new troll roared at us before running into the shadows. I frowned, watching it go, then saw the other trolls and goblins run into the woods.

"Gunther! Should we follow them?" Lord Adrijian asked.

Going on instinct alone, I shook my head. "No! They're heading into the trees. The shadow soldiers will ambush us."

Lord Adrijian nodded, but I still watched the cursed creatures go. This wasn't making any sense. Goblins were idiots when faced with a threat. They never retreated.

**"I'm checking the Rogue Narrator's code now, and it looks like the Dark Wizard is the biggest threat to these goblins. So, they need to obey him, or he... yep. Here. He incinerates them,"** Jim said.

What a delightful master.

**"I had notes about this. Jim, are you at the hospital?"** Devin asked.

**"No, I'm in my home office,"** Jim said.

Devin groaned, one that sounded suspiciously like someone climbing out of bed. **"Alright, it's time to admit when a man just won't get sleep. Give me about ten minutes and I'll get back with you on everything I know about goblins."**

Alright, thanks Devin.

"Were they coming after me?" Roger asked.

I glanced up at the man who still watched the retreating horde. "Sorry?"

"Me. Were they trying to kidnap me? When the soldiers failed, is that why they ran?"

His question made me uncomfortable. I didn't want to think about what might happen if the shadow soldiers kidnapped Roger. My inability to answer became the answer, and Roger's face turned to his default stoicism.

But the Rogue Narrator didn't need Roger in the Dark Wizard's grasp to change him. Unless he actually did. Was that what this was all about? Did the Dark Wizard need Roger near him to implant the new code?

**"It doesn't seem like he needs to. The Rogue Narrator could change him right now, but something tells me he wants you to see Roger turn, and then go after your characters to...."** I shook my head, trying to dispel the horrible thoughts conjured up by Jim's trailed off suggestion. **"Sorry."**

I also fought the urge to assure everyone that it wouldn't happen. My characters would be safe. I would *force* my characters to be safe.

**"Gunther."**

I know.

Roger looked at the retreating enemy before taking another large step back from the shadows. "Come on. We should make sure the seriously injured make it back to Tara and the other healers before nightfall."

My head bobbed from exhaustion, but it worked well enough as a nod.

That was an insane battle, Jim. Please tell me it took at least five thousand words.

**"You're inching closer to forty-eight thousand words total,"** Jim said.

Which means the Rogue Narrator still has about (I did the math on my fingers, only hesitating a little) twenty-two thousand words to do something to my characters. Right? Did my math work?

**"Yes. And twenty-two thousand is a lot better than seventy thousand. He may not do much more. You can always leave now."**

It was hard to describe, and more difficult to admit. In a few short days, Roger had won us all over. He was now part of my main group. Whatever the Rogue Narrator had planned for Roger, it would destroy his character worse than what would happen to Paldric, Tara, Milla, and Alwin. Whether or not the Rogue Narrator planned for this conclusion, it was the new reality I had to face.

I watched as Roger knelt, checking a man's wounds before asking him a question I couldn't hear. The injured man nodded, and Roger mumbled a joke to help the man smile.

Roger would never enjoy the database if the Rogue Narrator forced him to torture his friends. The Rogue Narrator had done it. He got me concerned about Roger like he was one of my characters, and the thought of that secret code altering this stoic man made my skin crawl.

The Rogue Narrator's character helped the injured man to his feet, making sure the man was steady before taking it slow toward the healers fanning out on the battlefield. I closed my eyes, my head hanging low. I can't leave yet, Jim. My stupid bleeding heart won't let me.

**"I understand,"** Jim said, his voice quiet with sympathy.

# Chapter Twenty-Five

# My Introspection Gets Me in Trouble With Everyone

We prepared for the inevitable evening attack. The shadows stretched as the sun sank closer to the horizon. In another hour or less, the shadows of Vaywell would touch the woods. Lord Adrijian and his head servant secured the manor house with the entire army inside. They lit multiple lanterns to make sure there were minimal shadows, despite the sun still in the sky. All my characters remained inside the manor house, including Milla. We tucked her away in a non-disclosed location for safekeeping.

There were people getting healed, people waiting to be healed, and people recovering from just being healed. It smelled of coppery blood mixed with the flowery scents of healing lotion. It was enough to want to open a window, but the threat was still there. No one dared suggest it, and I was glad Milla couldn't see this.

And then there was me, pacing back and forth, checking outside the window to see when the shadows would meet. I had my small section to pace near the wall, and I wore it out with my footfalls.

Devin hit me with a wall of info dumping that I'm summarizing now, even though I couldn't remember a lot.

**"Ouch, thanks Gunther. You know how much research went into that?"** Devin asked.

I appreciate the work you put into it. I really do. He had an entire file of those goblins' tragic back stories. Many of those goblins were now torn apart by the Siludontia and created a feast for the ocean floor. It almost made me feel guilty slaughtering them. Almost. They are still murdering monsters, set on killing any threat in their path. It helped me understand why they were crazy in the sun, with most of their torture being in the daytime. It made me realize how big of a threat the Dark Wizard was to them.

Roger walked up to me. I stopped my constant pacing. He folded his arms, leaning against the wall, and I triple checked to make sure his shadow was safe before allowing myself to relax.

"You should have Tara check that bruise." I tried to sound friendly as I noticed the blue and purple mark on his arm. "Make sure the bone isn't cracked."

"Yeah. I will. Later. There are people with more serious injuries waiting." Roger rubbed his bruise before wincing. If I pushed myself, I could figure out how he got the bruise and make a diagnosis.

**"It's not pushing yourself. It's using your God-powers. Don't make excuses,"** Devin said.

You're right. I shouldn't. Knowing my anxious state right now, only a tiny use of power would topple my sanity.

We fell silent again, the groaning and the quiet crying of the injured threatening to push my fried nerves over the edge. But I couldn't do anything. I couldn't.

**"We've got your back,"** Jim said.

My dried, tired eyes squeezed shut, my lids like sandpaper. I took my glasses off to stop a headache from forming.

I could… I could make everything not as—

**"Gunther,"** Jim and Devin both said.

Being alone with my thoughts was more dangerous than I wanted to admit.

Roger cleared his throat. "Thank you for saving my life back there."

I placed my glasses back on, sniffing. My hands shook, but I would use this time talking with Roger to keep myself from imagining all the ways I could stop this war. "A life for a life. I appreciate you returning the favor."

He said nothing, and our attention turned toward a man with a broken leg biting on a stick to keep him from shattering his teeth. The bone stuck out of his leg as multiple healers prepared to push it back. I turned away, trying to keep myself from dry heaving. Roger glanced at me. "I thought Gods would have stronger stomachs."

"This one doesn't." I fanned myself as the room turned warm. Sure, I had an epic battle between a dragon all ready to describe, but Alwin and Paldric's plot armor was firmly in place for it. Bruises, bumps, cuts, and slightly fragmented bones. In my story, the bone stayed well within the skin like they were supposed to.

"You don't look too good. Can I help?" Roger asked.

"Just nerves." I needed fresh air more than anything but was constricted by stupid laws someone else made up. This was going to drive me insane. "Let's just... talk. Talk to me."

Roger nodded. "I was actually... there's been something weighing on my mind. Would that be distracting enough?" I nodded, placing the back of my hand against my nostrils before staring at the ceiling. "Are you sure?"

"Give me a minute."

"Of course."

My fingers gripped my knees, realizing once again I was being an idiot in front of Roger. I took steadying, deep breaths before sliding down the wall, wiping the cold sweat from my forehead. Roger paused, then joined me on the ground. I placed the back of my head against the wall, sensing the fresh air just outside, but knowing I couldn't open a window. I would force myself to be okay if I needed to.

**"Gunther,"** Jim and Devin said again.

I closed my eyes. "Alright. What did you want to ask me?"

"Did you save me because you are a good person? Or did you save me because the evil God created me, and you didn't want me falling into his hands?"

I cracked an eye open. "Don't we always do things in our best interest? Isn't me saving you so the evil God doesn't force you to kill all these people in my best interest? And do you really think that's the only parameters for what we consider a good person?"

Roger sighed again, then held his arm against his chest. Yeah, Tara, or another healer, definitely needed to check that.

"Maybe that's what this all is. I hate how an evil God created me. I've never felt evil."

I kept my eyes mostly closed because of how squeamish I felt. But this conversation was a distraction from my long list of things I wanted to do to the Dark Wizard once I saw him again. "We're both in a similar situation, as much as I hate to admit it."

"We are?" Roger asked, confused.

I nodded, straightening. "I'd like to think I'm a good person, and yet I'm here, with unlimited power, trying not to crack. Far too willing to do things for my own selfish intentions."

"Like with Tara?" Roger asked.

"Like with Tara." I used every ounce of honesty I could convey in my tone.

"But you still have that choice. If you're right about me, I won't get one." Roger frowned, his eyes flitting over to Tara. I rubbed my upper arm, feeling uncomfortable. I didn't know what he was thinking, but I could guess. He already showed his dislike for me because of what I did to Tara, but with this secret code, Roger could do worse. That man would be miserable in the database, and he didn't deserve it. "You're quite certain he has a code all geared up for me to slaughter you all?"

"Why would he keep this a secret if it wasn't for this very reason? Or something similar?"

Roger folded his arms, making sure the bruise faced outwards. "But that's not like me."

"Yeah." It troubled me the moment I said it out loud. "You'd never hurt anyone. Just like I don't want to hurt anyone."

He raised an eyebrow at me. "But you've thought about it?"

I said nothing, keeping his gaze before closing my eyes again. I leaned against the wall, trying to put together a puzzle in my mind.

All of this, the war, the battle, it was too chaotic and made little sense. I expected some literary meaning, but the truth of the matter was, the Rogue Narrator didn't care about my story making sense. He just wanted to cause chaos. Chaos that would eventually break me. He did what he could to make me suffer. What could I have done in real life to cause such ire?

If the Rogue Narrator turned out to be my ex-wife, this would make more sense. What made me assume it wasn't her was because the Rogue Narrator had entered other stories. She wouldn't be that vicious to ruin other people's stories to make her look less suspicious. And I kind of hope Esme moved on with her life. She might have been this petty in the beginning, but I doubt she would have kept it up. Not this well.

**"We've already checked in on Esme. She's followed along the news stories, but she's no narrator. She couldn't pick out a narrator device even if there was a big sign pointing to it,"** Devin said.

I assumed as much. She never cared about my line of work. The only thing that threw me off was Roger's height. I'd kept it quiet for most of the book, but I couldn't any longer. Esme had this thing where she assumed I was super insecure about my height. I was almost six feet tall, and somehow it got into her head that anyone even a few inches taller must intimidate me somehow. I assured her I never cared, and yet she always insisted that meant I actually did care. It was a crazy mind game of hers that I never enjoyed playing, usually choosing to fall silent whenever she tried to mock how tall some men were. When Roger turned out to be a few inches taller than me, I thought it meant Esme was surely behind it. But nothing else made sense. It must have been a weird coincidence. A red herring, if you will.

My eyes traveled the length of the room as I straightened my glasses, glossing over the more disgusting injuries I refused to describe. I found Alwin and Paldric. They were talking, the worry clear on their faces. They thought about the next battle ahead. The enemy had us outnumbered, but we destroyed more than half of the goblins. The

Siludontia was happy and fat, swimming at the bottom of the ocean, more than willing to help tomorrow.

A bang at the wall rattled the windows. I partially sat up, realizing the shadows touched the woods. The shadow soldiers finally appeared.

My breath came out unsteadily. We assumed they would try, but all of us waited to see if they could break through. The lanterns and candles were enough to keep them at bay, but it was still unnerving. The shadow soldiers continued to beat against the wall, hissing as they stepped too close to the lights, either from the dying sun or from the lanterns.

I settled back against the wall, a hand through my hair. Paldric and Alwin sat across the room as a new, unsettling thought entered my mind. Roger asked me if I ever thought about hurting them, and truthfully, I didn't. But what would it take for me to hurt them?

The Guardians made it seem like the narrators snapped and started murdering all their creations. Maybe they wanted to paint them in a comically villainous light, because if things made sense to me—

**"Gunther,"** Jim said.

Then it would be more difficult to—

**"Stop that line of thinking right now, please,"** Jim said.

I paused, not daring to continue my thought, but I had to know. Comically terrible villains were only for stories. In real life, everyone had a reason for their choices. Roger turning evil and torturing everyone only made sense because we were in a story, but—

**"Gunther."** Devin's tone was hushed. **"Please."**

My gaze remained on Paldric and Alwin. What would be a logical reason to kill those two men over there? If the Rogue Narrator gained control of the story and turned Roger, killing my beloved characters would be a mercy. Kill them all before the Rogue Narrator altered their character so much that they would be miserable in the database.

A dagger appeared at my throat before I could react, and when I finally did, it was a sigh. "Honestly, Tara, this is weapon fatigue. You've placed a dagger at my throat so many times it's a pattern. You've got to shake things up, so readers think you're being seri—"

She pressed the dagger against my throat. The blade itself didn't cut off my speech, but I once again assumed she didn't want me to talk right now. "Why is your percentage in flux? And why do I know what flux means? And why are you thinking about killing Paldric and Alwin?" She said it so fast the three questions overlapped each other.

I glanced at my character, impressed at her ability to sneak up on me, and decided to not figure out how she did it, just in case she needed to do it again.

Roger stood up. "It's my fault. Gunther and I were chatting, and I mistakenly asked him if he ever thought about it."

She narrowed her eyes, and I could see the determination in her. If I was going to kill Paldric and Alwin, I would have to kill her first. That was how much she cared about those two guys. "Is it true, Gunther? Were you thinking about it in passing because Roger asked you about it?"

I remained sitting on the ground. "He asked me, and I thought about what kind of situation would require me to kill them."

"What situation would that be?" Tara dug the dagger deeper into my throat, which did not impede my speech at all, nor did it make a cut. She was undeterred by this lack of pain it caused me. "Tell me the truth, Gunther, because it will be better for everyone if you don't keep secrets from us."

My eyes betrayed me as I gave the barest glance in Roger's direction. Tara frowned. "So, his question made you think about their death?"

Roger kept his emotions in check. "No. He'd kill them if I ever fell into the Dark Wizard's control. If the secret code awakened in me."

Tara frowned, then looked at me for any sort of verbal confirmation. I said nothing, which was practically an affirmation. Her mouth dropped open, horrified.

"Wouldn't it be easier to kill me instead?" Roger sounded too calm for someone discussing his possible death.

Tara's eyes darted around as she got the information. "The percentage needed to kill any of us would give him a dangerous spike. It would be... be easier for Gunther to just kill us all. Death is easier than an altered character. He would do it before the world ended."

She was right. It would be better to have a quick death than to suffer through my insanity.

**"You're not going insane. Do you hear me? You can get out of the story now,"** Devin said.

If I kill them all before the Dark Wizard takes them, it fulfills my goal for them to remain who they are for the database.

**"Gunther—"** Jim said.

Hundreds of lanterns and candles went out at once, making me realize the sun had set for a while now. The silence lasted a second, even if it felt like an eternity, as we all realized just how dark it had become. Shadow soldiers threw open the doors and descended on us.

# Chapter Twenty-Six

# In My Epic Fantasy, I Forgot Magic Existed

I leapt to my feet. The shadow soldiers hissed and shrieked as they entered the manor house, and things turned chaotic again. This wasn't a place for a battle. The men weren't prepared; some of them didn't even have their swords near.

"Stop!"

It was a loud battle happening indoors, and I doubted anyone heard me over the din, yet I was. Shadow soldiers turned toward me, hissing, and one of them had a rock. Why was he holding a rock?

**"Oh, no."**

Oh, no? What oh no. What aren't you telling me, Devin?

**"I wasn't purposefully keeping this from you, but he is a wizard. I checked through his abilities again. He has the power to extinguish fires at command, like lanterns, and he can communicate with his minions through things like rocks."**

He's talking to the shadow soldiers right now? Is that why they are listening to me, somewhat?

**"Yep. The code just came in. That's the Dark Wizard ordering them about,"** Jim said.

If the Dark Wizard could hear me, that's probably why the shadow soldiers stalled the battle, waiting to see what I would do. Which is why I strode forward with all the confidence I didn't feel and put my hands in the air. "I give myself up!"

**"Um, Gunther? What are you doing?"** Jim asked.

We are in an enclosed space, and that shadow soldier is about to slit open a man's throat. It already reeks in here.

**"None of those reasons are good! What are you hiding?"** Devin asked.

"Please." I kept my hands in the air. "Leave these good people alone. You only want me."

**"Gunther, you still have..."** Jim paused, most likely calculating my word count. **"You have about twenty**

**thousand words left. Now is not the time to do something like this."**

If I can distract him long enough, my other characters can run to safety.

**"In twenty *thousand* words?"** Devin asked.

My reply was forming on my tongue, even though it seemed like I was stalling because I didn't have a proper reply, but I had one. Just forming the words I needed for my response. Right about now. They're coming.

The Dark Wizard's voice came through the rock, loud enough for all to hear. "These are images of the individuals I want. Drag them to our camp. Kill anyone who stops you."

Despite my lack of knowledge of the Rogue Narrator's code, I had a good idea whose images the Dark Wizard sent. The atmosphere of the room stirred with general feelings of unease as injured men rose, prepared once again to battle. At least Milla was still hid—

"Gunther!" Milla shouted behind me, on the verge of tears. "Why have all the lanterns gone out?"

I pursed my lips, closed my eyes, and bowed my head. Oh, this little girl was not prepared to have more emotional trauma. Or ever, really. In a perfect world, Milla would have no more trauma, and she would live with Tara and

Paldric forever. Let me pause the drama and describe this perfect world for the next twenty thousand words.

Is it working?

**"Nope."** Devin sounded annoyed.

A shadow soldier grabbed my arms as other men tried to come to my aid.

"No, don't!" I searched for Lord Adrijian and locked eyes with him. "Keep the men back. I have a plan. Alright? No one else needs to die tonight."

**"What's your plan?"** Devin asked.

I have no idea whatsoever. Don't tell my characters.

Devin groaned as Lord Adrijian lifted a hand to stop the soldiers. I hoped the Dark Wizard would take just me, but a big, nasty villain wouldn't lose an opportunity like this. Tara glared as shadow soldiers grabbed her arms, and Roger gave me another stoic look as shadow soldiers surrounded him. The soldiers' grip felt cold and damp, somehow, but not the relaxing cool of a pleasant shade on a warm summer day. More the shadow in the wintertime, coupled with the dread of knowing it would only get colder.

What hurt was when two shadow soldiers scooped Milla up, who shrieked in fear. Roger's stoic look turned into a glare as the surrounding soldiers took out their swords.

"It's alright. Milla, it's going to be alright! It's all according to plan!"

Shadow soldiers started dragging my main group of characters (and Roger) out of the manor house. Tara glared at me. "You better be right about this, or I'm going to murder you."

Roger shook his head. "Best wait in line, Tara."

Once we were out of the manor house, Paldric and Alwin joined us, both keeping a strong eye on the shadow soldiers holding Milla. The creatures had her in the air to keep up with the rest of us. She wanted to kick them where she sometimes kicked her brothers when they were being cruel, but she couldn't reach. Milla closed her eyes as we passed through the city and toward the moat, past the bodies of soldiers, goblins, and trolls.

Alwin wanted to break free, but turned toward me instead. "Are you sure you know what you're doing?"

**"Answer Alwin's question. And be honest,"** Devin said.

Be honest? You want me to tell them everything? About how this is nothing more than a story we're all part of. How these people are nothing more than figments of my imagination? Brought to life using extremely high-tech virtual reality?

**"Then let me clarify. Please stop hiding things from us. It'll only get you into deeper trouble. We need you to be honest, or we won't be able to help you,"** Devin said.

My lips formed a tight line before the words tumbled from my mouth. "I don't know what I'm doing, no." My eyes remained ahead, so I didn't have to look at anyone. The moat receded into the distance. "I am usually such an architect with this sort of thing, but ever since coming here, it's been nothing but streams of consciousness and gardening. I am bad at both, and it causes me anxiety."

"None of that makes sense." There was the slightest touch of anger in Alwin's tone, which meant my elf was livid. "Be clear for once in your life. We are being dragged to the Dark Wizard's camp, and it cannot be good."

"I have a plan. A vague one. There's been no time to workshop it, and I'm terrified it's going to fail, but I owe it to myself to try."

"And if it fails?" Alwin asked.

When I looked at my elf's face, I didn't need to answer his question. Paldric, who was next to Alwin, wondered if this was the night all of us would die.

Which wasn't the greatest of comforts. The guy known for optimism didn't simply have the thought and let it flit away. No, it remained, and he formed his plan to protect Milla and Tara to his last breath.

The Dark Wizard's camp was closer than I thought as a bonfire came into view. Other creatures surrounded it. I thought of what this would've been like if a troll or goblin did the capturing and subsequent dragging through the battlefield. We were right to not obliterate the species the other night.

Please tell me that internal dialogue translated to twenty thousand words of pure poetry.

**"You don't even have enough to finish this chapter,"** Devin said.

Oh, I'll finish it. I've got to keep this as detail heavy as I can.

**"Gunther—"** Devin said.

There were too many trolls and goblins for my liking. Even after the battle this afternoon, it still felt daunting how many cursed creatures stood on the edge of the bonfire's light. Shadow soldiers dragged goblins who got too close to the firelight, both of them hissing at each other. Though the goblins were more docile at night, the bonfire still agitated them. The shadow soldiers didn't want them going crazy and causing another fight. The air was thick with the anticipation of another battle breaking out, whether between us or between the members themselves.

Despite the shadow soldiers letting us go as soon as the light of the fire illuminated our surroundings, my legs still moved without my command. It was dark magic. Though I knew the Dark Wizard was magical, I didn't know how he got this level of enchantment in my story. My magic system was more of a decay. Of using what was swiftly running out. The Dark Wizard had a source somewhere, most likely from the Rogue Narrator.

Paldric struggled against the power. Tara gasped before dropping to her knees, her hands pinned magically behind her. I felt the pressure too, and I tried not to fight it, though it did a number on my knees when they smacked the ground. A few months more, and I'd be thirty. I heard about what turning thirty does to one's knees. Dark magic forced my wrists behind my back, almost like they were powerful magnets. Roger collapsed on his knees next to me, facing my characters stationed behind me. I tried not to think that the Dark Wizard positioned him this way to make it easier for his killing spree. I wouldn't let that happen.

It was hard to see through the many trolls and goblins surrounding us. They snarled at the six of us, waiting for permission to rip us apart. But they grew fearful, and I had a feeling I knew why.

The fire was hot against one side of my face as a path formed through the goblins and trolls. I sensed my characters preparing for whatever came, and… and most of them hoped I wasn't as idiotic as they feared.

I couldn't help but look over my shoulder. "Hey!" They glanced at me. The confusion was obvious on their faces. "I mean, I sort of have a plan. It doesn't make me an idiot, but I'm trying."

My words did nothing to comfort them.

**"You now have about eighteen thousand words left,"** Jim said.

That was too many words, considering the situation we found ourselves in.

**"You mean the situation you put yourself in? And dragged your other characters into?"** Devin asked.

Maybe I really was an idiot.

The Dark Wizard walked through the cleared pathway. I watched him appear in the bonfire light. He was tall, and it wasn't because I was on my knees. If I had to guess, he was at least six and a half feet, with flowing black hair and a beard. He had eyes so brown they almost looked black. He held a black staff, and leaned against it, acting like an old man, and yet… not? The more I studied him, the more I couldn't figure it out. He didn't have any gray in his hair. His face looked ageless, and yet in that agelessness

I couldn't sense youth. Youth had a sense of carefree or innocence mingled with it. This guy looked how I felt. Laden with responsibilities of adulthood with the slightest bitter feeling about it. But his skin looked great.

Jim snorted at my internal comment, but I'm right, wouldn't you say? This man does not look a day over thirty.

**"He has marvelous skin, yes. Probably more dark magic,"** Jim said.

Or he exfoliates. That's a thing in the real world, right? I heard Esme talking about it. A lot.

The Dark Wizard had no smile on his face as he opened his mouth. "Yes, exfoliating is a thing in the real world. Not that I need it here."

Which is when I realized he could read my thoughts with him being controlled by the Rogue Narrator. My thoughts returned to how much I felt like an idiot.

The Dark Wizard brushed off his robe. "You are, yes."

"At least I didn't ruin my grand entrance by stating my thoughts on exfoliating. My creations are more confused now, rather than terrified," I mumbled.

He glared. "Shall we talk instead of your idiotic maneuvers and your stupid plans of heroism that never work."

I winced as I felt the gaze of every single one of my characters and sensed their fear. But I still... still sorta had... had a plan.

# Chapter Twenty-Seven

# I Am, Without a Doubt, an Idiot

The Dark Wizard gave me a humorous look. "Right."

I tried to think of something to stretch this conversation to pad the word count. "Look, Mr. Wizard, we've got to agree on something."

He pulled a cloth from his pocket before shooting it magically through the air right into my mouth. There was a grimy feeling to it that my mouth wanted to reject. Before I could spit it out, another cloth, also not clean, wrapped around my mouth to keep it there and tied itself behind my head. I groaned, fighting down the need to dry heave as the grimy cloth moved and something I could only describe as slime collected onto my tongue.

The Dark Wizard's smile was still noticeably absent from his face. "Go ahead. Clean the cloth. Make it so you don't taste the goblin sweat and the troll puss."

I crumpled in on myself at his words, and before I could stop myself, the rag cleaned itself.

Tara hissed, not wanting to bring attention to herself, but needing to at the same time ever since I transferred powers over to her. "Fifty-eight."

**"Steady, Gunther."** Jim said it like I was some sort of horse.

"Tell that goody-two shoes Jim he won't win this time," the Dark Wizard said.

Despite the lame insult the Rogue Narrator tried to give Jim, I was more focused on my situation, while also trying to block myself from thinking about it. I should have forced the gag off myself with my powers, but I cleaned it instead. I teetered on a dangerous slope. My powers couldn't be used any more than I had to.

**"Never. You never use your powers. Understand?"** Devin asked.

The Dark Wizard chuckled, still with no smile on his face. "Oh, I will make him use his powers."

Okay, can everyone just stop reading my thoughts? It's super overwhelming right now.

The Dark Wizard moved past me to my characters as I tried to think of a plan. Couldn't he be a monologuing villain, so I could trick him into adding more to my word count? Except if I thought about my plan to get him to talk, then the Dark Wizard would know.

Which meant I already tipped him off.

"My master has done this for a while now. He is fast. Efficient. He can break your characters in less time than the necromancer could give the monologue you desire."

I breathed more heavily, blinking ahead at the goblins and trolls surrounding us. Focusing on the little things to keep my terror at bay and pad my word count. The way the torchlight moved with the wind. The troll slobber gleaming in the light of the fires. Beady black eyes from the goblins as they stared at me with deep hatred. Cracked and worn weapons dangerous enough to crush my characters' skulls.

None of this helped.

"So good to see you again, Tara." The Dark Wizard took out a dagger and placed the blade under her chin to lift her head. "I see none of my former lessons have stuck. We'll have to continue them."

"No!" Paldric shouted.

"Over my dead body!" Roger said at the same time.

The Dark Wizard chuckled again. I closed my eyes, doing as little as possible so the device didn't find me interesting. If the Dark Wizard wanted to monologue, he could be my guest.

"Shall we play this game, Gunther? Shall I break the will of your characters, so they completely hate you? Hate the person who created them? I've never done that before. This will be such a *novel* experience." I rolled my eyes. "Stop me with your powers whenever you wish. I'm sure you'd like to see the world burn before another person figures out the real you and leaves."

I refused to react to his insult.

"Don't lie to everyone. We can all clearly see you squirming," the Dark Wizard said.

Would it matter if my characters hated me? Would it affect their experience in the database? As long as it didn't drastically alter their characters. All of them seemed to hate me a little, and they were still who they were.

The Dark Wizard placed his dagger against Paldric's throat, way too close for my liking. "You tell me, as his creator, what would Paldric become after he hated you? How could he keep his optimism when he came to detest the man who created him?"

My mind froze. I refused to follow that villain's train of thought. Scenes of a bitter Paldric threatened to leap into existence. I refused to give the Rogue Narrator the satisfaction.

"Alright." The Dark Wizard sheathed his dagger. "We'll just find out for ourselves, shall we?"

I closed my eyes and bowed my head. I guess we would.

"Oh, it'll be easy. And it concerns you." The Dark Wizard stood in front of Milla, who had quiet tears down her cheeks. She was between Paldric and Tara and tried to curl into herself. An eight-year-old couldn't handle this. Roger squirmed next to me.

"You're right, Gunther. It's too much for an eight-year-old." The Dark Wizard got down on one knee, and Milla tried to move closer to Paldric as best she could, but all of us were stuck on our knees. It didn't stop Paldric from trying to get to her, too. To break the dark magic that kept his wrists together. The Dark Wizard finally smiled. "Don't you think your original plans for her would have worked better? Don't you think she's gone through enough trauma? This is no place for an eight-year-old. It would have been better if she had died when Pavaldri killed her. When *you* wanted her dead."

Milla gasped. Paldric frowned, not believing a word of what the Dark Wizard said. Tara looked at the back of my head as I lowered it. It was enough for her to believe it. I didn't know what Roger thought of me, but his shocked expression couldn't be good. However, it was Alwin's unsettled nature that shocked me more than I expected. I acted like his people. The elves who left mankind to their own devices, even though I saved Milla. But Alwin didn't care. He realized how dangerous it was for anyone to be a God. For anyone to have this much power over another. He realized he had a portion of this power over humans, and it disgusted him.

Alwin, supportive side character, was the first to start turning against me, and hinting at his own dark arc.

"Wouldn't that bring an interesting dynamic?" The Dark Wizard stared right at Alwin. "The faithful friend, always in the background, finally getting the arc he deserves. To go insane with power. Just like you should do, Gunther. Is it any surprise your own desires manifested in one of your creations?"

I said nothing. Did nothing. Thought nothing.

"Gunther's a changed man. He wouldn't kill her now. In fact, there were plenty of times Milla could have died, and he saved her," Paldric said.

"Oh, right. It's a matter of who he kills you're concerned with," the Dark Wizard said.

Paldric glared at the ageless man, hoping to keep his focus away from Milla. "What are you talking about?"

"Just my minions." My heart rate spiked. "As long as Gunther doesn't kill Milla and instead kills my cursed creatures, that's really all you're concerned about." Paldric said nothing. Instead, he furrowed his brows, watching the Dark Wizard. "You don't know them, do you? No one ever cared to. They just saw ugly faces and deemed them evil."

"They ransacked villages. Kidnapped Tara. They were ready to kill the men of Vaywell City," Paldric said.

"Because they were banished. Cursed. Told that what they are is evil. Never given time to develop, just like every other villain in any other world. You just need them to be vaguely evil enough to justify murdering them." The Dark Wizard turned to Tara. "You needed to be enough of a beautiful blank slate for Gunther to believe he was justified in assaulting you." Tara stared, wide eyed. "Your God is a murderer and a rapist, who even in his throne in the heavens had blood on his hands. He didn't care about your welfare, he only cared about being entertained. Milla's life had no value until he decided it did. My minions, who have been banished by his people—" the Dark Wizard gestured at Alwin, "—didn't know their worth. They are doing what they can. I assure you; it will be all of you who become monsters and demons and childhood horrors of my creations when we win this war. After your annihilation. It's all a matter of perspective."

The Dark Wizard stood in front of me. I kept my gaze lowered. "Wouldn't you agree, Gunther?"

I was smiling. The gag was hiding it, but since the Rogue Narrator, and therefore the Dark Wizard, could read my thoughts, he knew what the gag hid. The Dark Wizard gave me a curious look. "What's so funny?"

Oh, this was satisfying. I got you monologuing! And it worked! Not that it padded the word count much, but because I caught a glimpse of the real you. Do you know how long it took me to figure this out? I deserve a monologue of my own.

The Dark Wizard pulled out his sword, prepared for anything, eyes narrowed. I stared back at him, my smile as sure as ever.

Hello, Professor Andrews. It feels so good to finally unmask you.

# Chapter Twenty-Eight

# UNRELIABLE NARRATOR DOES HIS BEST TO BE RELIABLE AGAIN

Yes, the revelation would've been cooler with a more literary approach. Sprinkled hints of Professor Andrews here and there, weaved him into the story, plant multiple red herrings and not just my ex-wife. Something so that people who didn't know Professor Andrews in real life still remembered him. Instead of when I said his name... twice? Possibly three times? I don't quite remember, but that proves my point. This was real life. It didn't get the dramatic flair I hoped, but I didn't care. I just felt relief it was done.

Devin and Jim gasped. I kept my smirk there, fully hidden by the gag, but the Dark Wizard (the Rogue Narrator, Professor Andrews) knew it was there.

**"Wait, wait, wait. What?"** Devin asked.

**"Are you certain?"** Jim asked.

Not only that, but I remember now. Roger's height *was* important. Not because I was insecure about it, but because Esme was there at that narration dinner for seniors and tried to belittle me about my height in front of someone else. But you heard her, Professor Andrews. You checked up on me privately the next day in class to make sure I was okay. You were trying to be nice, but you must have logged it away. Made it so I thought Esme created Roger. Didn't you?

The Dark Wizard blinked, then glanced around, frowning. What do you expect from an insecure man with a nonexistent smile, and when it does, it's slimy? The man has delusional ideas because he doesn't realize how close he is to death.

He still looked confused, his hand tightening over his sword before returning his gaze to me.

That's what I thought. Professor Andrews cut his connection with the Dark Wizard. His character can't read my thoughts anymore, which means the man is running.

**"Devin, call Vince. I'll call the authorities at the university to alert them. He can't have run far."**

**"We're going to disconnect to make some calls, but we're still monitoring your story. You haven't told me how you figured this out."**

Yeah, I know. I'm sorry, Devin, but I had to be sure. Let me figure out how to provide the wall of text to help you understand what I did.

**"You're not using your powers, are you?"**

It shouldn't take up time, because the device should already have it written up how I discovered this. Professor Andrews gave a lecture about the perspective of your villain in my collage class ages ago and it was the final piece of my puzzle. The guy cannot help but start lecturing when he needs to get his say.

**"Don't flashback, Gunther. You can't risk having us not see what's going on,"** Jim said.

I'll provide a mountain of text to go through while I'm sitting here so you can see I'm not hiding anything. This will boost my word count nicely! Here you go:

The moment the Rogue Narrator revealed himself back in book one, I got the impression he would be someone I knew. That, or someone I met recently, like the Guardians. But I stifled my thoughts, because the last thing I needed was for him to get tipped off I was onto them. Yes, my staying here was about saving my characters, but if I was one hundred percent honest, I wanted to unmask the guy.

When Roger appeared as a character, it gave me an idea. I could use him to figure out if the Rogue Narrator was someone I knew. I'd listen to Roger for familiar anecdotes or turns of phrases that might be from people in my life. But it was hard. So many other things distracted me. The safety of my characters, personally, was always on my mind, even as I was doing this dangerous primary mission.

The night of the ball changed everything. Roger convinced the Rogue Narrator to stop the attack, even if he didn't realize it. He became his own character, just like every narrator wanted. Which meant I would never discover the Rogue Narrator's identity by asking Roger questions. I needed to go straight to the source. To the Dark Wizard himself.

And how did I figure this all out without tipping the Guardians off? Well, Devin was right. I knew exactly why the three percent increase happened (it was a beast to keep hidden from you, Devin. You are inquisitive and don't let things go).

As I pretended to sleep on the night of the ball, I hatched a plan and made sure no one knew about it. I weighed the pros and cons and knew it would hurt my sanity. However, discovering the Rogue Narrator's identity was the only thing I would sacrifice my characters for. I didn't want other narrators stuck in my same situation. So, I hid my percentage rise from Tara, and I had the device work with me to figure out the identity of the Rogue Narrator. The device listed potential candidates based on my knowledge and experiences. It surprised me to discover Professor Andrews near the top. Esme was, of course, near the top, too, but it made little sense for her to be there. I kept it from the Guardians because all of you were on the list, with Devin being closest to Esme and Professor Andrews. I'm sorry, Devin, but I had to be sure.

The three percent hike needed to be acknowledged, but I didn't let Tara know about it until morning, then did my best to pretend I didn't know. I couldn't even think about it with all of you reading my thoughts. Devin was way too close to the top to confide in him, and I couldn't confide in Jim, Grace, or Vince, in case it got back to Devin. Not only that, the other Guardians were still on the list, which meant I couldn't trust any of them until they fell off. And none of you did.

I spent the next two days doing everything I could to remain reliable and innocent. Prepare for the war, fight hard enough to be a threat, and allow us to get captured because then I could meet the Rogue Narrator face to face. And when he started giving that lecture about a villain's point of view, I knew exactly who he was. Well, okay, not exactly, but I did that test to see if he was running, and he did.

Isn't it odd, Professor Andrews, that you always felt so sympathetic for villains in a person's story? Except you're not reading this right now because you're being chased by the authorities. Gotcha!

**"Oh, this isn't long. Maybe two pages worth of text,"** Devin said.

Really? You mean it isn't thousands of words long? I'm not nearing the end of book two?

**"Yeah, it barely added another six hundred words to your count."**

I deflated. Keeping Devin unaware was exhausting, and I hoped revealing my plan would somehow translate into a long monologue. I guess not.

**"I'm going to read it right now, while I call Vince. Jim's still on the line with the authorities. We're going to catch him."**

It meant there were too many words left, and we were still stuck in the middle of the Dark Wizard's camp. I stared at the moon above me. Despite my need to unmask the Rogue Narrator, I hoped my characters would come out of this only a little scathed. Yeah, alright, I hoped this would end with me giving my monologue. Then I would bow and disappear before ending the story. But as Jim and Devin pointed out, I still needed about seventeen thousand words. There was no way I could make a monologue that long.

The Dark Wizard struck me on the head with the sword hilt. I shouted first from surprise, then groaned as the pain caught up with me. It was my fault for lowering my guard. I thought with Professor Andrews not controlling his character, he wouldn't be much of a threat. He was still a villain, though.

"Gunther!" The concern was so obvious in Roger's voice that I knew it was genuine. I tried to scramble away, but dark magic still connected my knees to the ground. The Dark Wizard hit me again with the hilt.

Paldric couldn't break the bonds, but he was still going to try. "Stop it!"

"You think you have the makings of a hero?" The Dark Wizard released my knees from the ground, so when he kicked my face, I landed on my back, blood spurting from my broken nose. I let out a muffled scream.

I didn't expect this. Maybe I should have. Evil people get angry when thwarted.

"I don't need to torture your characters to make you break." He kicked my stomach over and over. Paldric would tear his hands off to get me, as Roger shouted my name. Tara screamed at the Dark Wizard to stop it, and Milla sobbed. Alwin was desperately finding some way to rescue me. "I was going to make them hate you, but this will work just as well." He kicked me right in the balls, and I somehow felt them in my stomach. I almost swallowed the gag as I squealed. "I simply have to cause you enough pain before you can't handle it anymore. Then you can be the one to kill your characters."

My body demanded I get rid of the debilitating pain. I could, if I wanted to. My nausea made me far too aware of the gag in my mouth. The constant sharp pain forced me to curl into myself, to hide, to hope that the fetal position would dispel the hurt.

The Dark Wizard went to kick me in the balls again when I grabbed his foot. His slimy smile appeared before I realized why. I couldn't grab his foot unless my hands were free of his powers. Something that could only happen if I used my own. It felt like waking up from a nightmare; the pain eased away, the nausea with it.

"Fifty-nine," Tara said.

No, that wasn't accurate. I'm sorry, everyone, I swear this is my final revelation. The pain disappeared, my nose snapped back into place and the blood returned inside my body before the wounds sealed shut. I released the block I snuck onto Tara's abilities that night, and finally let her see my real percentage.

Tara gasped, her eyes wide in terror. "Gunther! You're at a hundred and thirty-seven percent!"

The cloth keeping the gag inside my mouth untied itself. I spat the rag out, my fingers still gripping the Dark Wizard's foot. "Not nearly as bad as I thought."

<u>Chapter Twenty-Nine</u>

# I Am Not Insane

"**G**unther!" There was no denying the anger in Devin's voice now. **"What have you done!"**

I'm sorry again. Honestly. I didn't plan on telling you until I was out of my story, but nothing is pulling the word count I expected. And the Dark Wizard had a nasty idea about me and pain.

**"Get out now. Do you hear me? Get out!"** There was concern under the anger. But I couldn't go yet. **"Yes, you can! You've done what you came here to do, and you're... you're past..."**

"Gunther." Tara was almost breathless, the terror as clear in her voice as the anger in Devin's. "Why?"

It was a simple question, one I had a simple answer to, but my characters wouldn't get it. "I needed to keep the heavens safe."

It was because of you, Devin. You would have the power to change my plot once I hit sixty percent, and you were still too high on my list.

**"Oh, this is bad. Get out, Gunther."**

Not yet. A final thing needed to be solved.

**"You had a choice between unmasking the Rogue Narrator or saving your characters. You made your choice. Get out now!"** Devin said.

The Dark Wizard smiled like everything was going according to plan before he threw his hand out, his glowing purple finger pointed right at Roger's chest. I matched his speed, creating an invisible force field only I and the Dark Wizard sensed. Roger glanced behind his shoulder, saw me holding something invisible at bay, and tried to back away. But his knees were still bound to the ground like everyone else. I wasn't bound, but still on my knees, panting as I held back the Dark Wizard's power.

The code, Devin. The Dark Wizard is activating the secret code in Roger. I've paused it long enough. Tell me what's in it.

Tears formed in Tara's eyes. "One hundred and thirty-eight."

Devin?

**"Get out of the story. It's not worth it. Get out while you're not aware of what you've done."**

Decode it, or I will.

"One hundred and thirty-nine," Tara whispered.

Paldric stared at Tara, his jaw dropping before he looked at me, trying to take Milla's hand. Roger, a man whose thoughts I could not read, kept his eyes closed and braced himself, waiting for the code to manifest.

**"It was your characters or unmasking the Rogue Narrator. You cannot do both. Get out of your story. I'm begging you."**

**"This is Jim, logging on again."** His tone was far too calm for the current situation. **"Hey, man, I'm going to decode this as fast as possible, but I need you to take a step back with me."**

"One hundred and forty." Tara barely said it, but everyone heard it.

**"Remember, this is a story. It's been a wild ride, but every narrator knows when they get in too deep,"** Jim said.

How do I know you're working on decoding it and not doing something else?

**"I've decoded the Rogue Narrator's stuff so much I can almost do it in my sleep."**

I sensed Jim working on the code hanging in the air near Roger's head, waiting to touch him so it could activate.

The man beside me looked helpless, with his head bowed and eyes closed.

**"Do you ever have those times when creating a world that you're completely lost in it?"** His voice remained calm as the layers of code peeled back. **"So stuck in world building and character development that everything else seems bland in comparison?"**

My eyes narrowed as the Dark Wizard continued to push. We were in a virtual tug of war, and Jim was talking me down. But I couldn't let that code hit Roger without me knowing what was in it. I could still protect my characters. Protecting Roger was the last piece I needed to stop Professor Andrews. I may be over one hundred percent, but I was an anomaly. I've lasted longer in my story than anyone, and I will be the one who lasts past one hundred percent.

"One hundred and forty-one."

This needed to end, but not without understanding the code.

**"I'm almost there, Gunther. I promise. Just understand how deep you've gone. Life isn't bland. It's real. So are books. Narrators are so full of life they want to create more. If you're serious about your craft, you've got to know when to let go. You can't be a good**

**creator of worlds without experiencing the real one first. We want you to come back."**

"One hundred and forty-two."

**"You are a good person, just like Roger. I believe in you. It doesn't matter that Professor Andrews created him. You know how dangerous this device is, and you will make the right choice. You will get out. I know it."**

Jim pressed the code into my mind, and I blinked. Probably the first blink I made this entire tug of war. I sensed every aspect of what it would do to Roger. It was as I feared. Not just kill, he would torture, rape, destroy. Do whatever he could to alter my characters. He'd become no better than the goblins in sunlight. This urge would overwhelm him, destroying his previous character codes, so this became the dominant one.

I turned to see Roger kneeling next to me. He had his eyes open again, watching this virtual tug of war, tears in his eyes. He caught my gaze, and I sensed the terror his character felt. No, I didn't sense it because I wasn't his narrator. I simply understood. He wouldn't want this. He would never murder Milla, or rape Tara, or torture Paldric and Alwin, because it wasn't in his character. That's not the man I knew. The misery he'd feel in the database was something I couldn't stand by and watch. Despite how insensitive and, admittedly, downright cruel I had been to him, he was still good. And I already knew the best thing to do about this code.

My eyes closed, touching the code to make one specific change. This would not destroy who he was, because my story wouldn't allow it. My characters stayed consistent with who they were. Basic rules of my story made radical shifts in character forbidden.

In other words, I gave Roger the thing he wanted most. A choice.

"One hundred and forty-five."

I dropped my hand. The altered code hit Roger in the back. He gasped, curling in on himself. My back hit the ground, and I hugged my legs, taking a few deep breaths, my stomach in knots from anxiety and stress. Tara warned me she would kill me if I ever hit ninety. I could already sense her plan.

The Dark Wizard smiled, then released his hold on Roger. I touched my side, staring at the ground, everything hitting me all at once. A hundred percent with over ten thousand words left to go. Roger received the code from the Rogue Narrator.

From Professor Andrews. The man who I learned the art of storytelling. The man who helped me and countless others get degrees. Brought my stories to life even without the device. He didn't seem like a backstabber. Never force me to teeter on the edge of losing my sanity. But there were memories that came back with terrifying clarity.

He stated at the beginning of class that most villains people wrote were two dimensional. He guaranteed fleshing them out would instead turn the villain into the hero. Discussions where he was firmly on the side of characters being the lesser creations. How they weren't as important as people in real life, and he assured us all he wasn't a psychopath for believing it. Somehow, it was the assurance of normalcy that made me the most uneasy.

**"We're here for you. Come back. It'll be alright. You can slam the prison door to Professor Andrews' cell yourself if you'd like. You just have to be in this world when you do,"** Jim said.

The Dark Wizard helped Roger to his feet before handing him a sword. "Hurt them. However way you wish. However gruesome. Make it happen."

Roger frowned, studying the sword in his hands, before looking at the Dark Wizard. Relief flooded my system. A part of me was suspicious that Roger was leading me down a path full of false security, but I knew him. A man who treated me with undeserved kindness. Eye contact was unnecessary. Roger would not murder my characters.

The Dark Wizard narrowed his eyes. With no connection to Professor Andrews, he wouldn't understand I altered the code. "Slit Paldric's throat now, Roger."

With unknown speed, Roger shoved the blade toward the Dark Wizard's chest. The vile man moved with the momentum, gasping in shock, but the blade never pierced him. Roger might as well have stabbed a brick wall. He lost his grip on the hilt, groaning as the blade clattered to the ground. He brought his hand to him, staring at the perfectly whole chest in surprise.

The Dark Wizard looked disappointed. "Do you honestly think I'd come to a battle and not be prepared?"

The armor artifact. Of course he would. I went through the different things to do that wouldn't push me over the edge, starting with freeing everyone from his enchantment. Alwin, already sensing it, leapt to his feet.

**"You are already over the edge. Get out of your story. The code in Roger is harmless. When you admitted to being over a hundred percent, I already sent Lord Adrijian to your position. Help is already on its way,"** Jim said.

There are too many words left, and my characters—

**"You are past one hundred percent, and I fully believe your characters can take care of themselves. Back me up here, Devin."**

A dagger bounced off my torso, and I looked up with enough time to see Tara next to me, somehow in possession of a sword. Despite the Dark Wizard standing right there, she was glaring at me. "You lied."

"I had to do—"

"No, you didn't," Tara said.

**"Devin?"** Jim asked.

"You didn't have to do anything. Now you've put us all in danger!" Tara shouted.

**"When was the last time you've heard from Devin?"** The calmness finally disappeared, and there was panic in Jim's voice.

Arrows flew overhead as Lord Adrijian's army descended on us. Milla ignored Tara and her sword. She went on instinct and ran to me. With that same instinct, I covered her with my body to keep her safe from the battle we found ourselves in.

"We don't have time for this!" I shouted at Tara. "Go help the others!"

"No!" Her hand was still on the hilt of her sword. "You are the most dangerous person right now."

Paldric, Alwin, and Roger joined the battle, fighting any cursed creatures that got too close. I glared at Tara. There were too many times that woman pressed daggers against my throat. She didn't know how to kill me. No one did. I couldn't die in this world.

**"Gunther, get out of your story and check on Devin. I'm not at the hospital where he is. I'm getting there as fast as I can, but he's not responding to his calls. You've got to figure out what's going on."**

I am literally in the middle of another battle. The Dark Wizard is getting away, and I need to keep my characters safe.

**"Devin and I are in real life, and he's in danger right now! Please, Gunther. Get out. I don't like this at all!"**

My glare was still pointed at Tara, and she took the smallest step back, her eyes narrowing. "What are you thinking?"

"Stop pretending you know how to kill me. Stop pointing a sword at me like it's going to save you."

Milla let go, looking at me with wide, frightened eyes. Tara grabbed her shoulder, backing her away from me.

"Gunther?" the little girl asked.

I blinked, staring at her ridiculously large brown eyes. A lifetime ago, I chose her to be my gauge because I couldn't foresee a time when I would kill her, and I forced myself to keep looking at her. Forced myself to wonder if I was at that point now.

"One hundred and forty-four," Tara whispered.

**"Yes, this is an emergency! I need you to check room four twenty-three. Devin is not responding. Is he alright?"** Jim asked, most likely into a phone.

Lord Adrijian's army chased the goblins and the trolls. The Dark Wizard ran, inspiring his cursed creatures to do the same.

Alwin appeared, trying to be silent, but I saw him straight off. He abandoned the battle to help Tara if needed. He kept the arrow notched in his bow pointed to the ground as he approached with fresh injuries on his face.

"I'm fine." A headache formed behind my eyes, but they didn't need to know that. "No one is in danger because of me. I promise."

**"I'm pulling into the parking lot now! What happened! Is Devin alright!"**

Roger and Paldric approached too, watching me carefully. Roger held his shoulder, blood dripping from a cut there. In fact, blood stained the ground. He was badly hurt, and it was an excellent distraction for me.

I got to my feet. "Lay down, Roger. You're hurt." They did nothing, still ready to kill me if Tara gave the word. "Come on, guys, I won't hurt any of you. Roger, sit down before you pass out. You can't have lost that much blood and still be on your feet."

They said nothing, and I didn't understand why until I noticed Milla, covered in blood. My heart leapt to my throat. She wasn't in the battle. Why was there blood all over her dress? It seemed like she just noticed it herself. Paldric, next to Milla, stared wide eyed at my stomach. It was then I noticed my hand, which was pointed toward Roger, covered in blood. I looked down to see a modern hospital scalpel sticking out of my gut.

"Oh."

# Chapter Thirty

# WE WRAP UP BOOK TWO

What I thought was anxiety in my stomach was something else entirely. Something far more permanent.

**"Get out! Get out of your story now!"** Jim shouted.

Code 0000. I leave my story. Immediately. I leave immediately.

I looked at my characters. They stared at me wide eyed. They were still here. I wasn't leaving.

"I leave. I leave my story. Please."

My adrenaline left instead. Blood trickled from my mouth.

**"What's going on? Why haven't you left?"**

I'm trying, Jim. I swear I am.

My knees gave out, and Alwin and Paldric caught me. They eased me onto my back to keep the scalpel from digging deeper into my stomach. Though, maybe it wouldn't, because this wasn't real life. I wasn't in real life. I was stuck in my story. Again.

Paldric turned toward Tara, a pleading look in his eyes. "Can you do something?"

Tara was at my side.

Code 0000. I leave. I'm leaving. Please let me leave.

Air struggled to enter my lungs as I stared at the moon, with the stars covering the sky. Paldric helped Tara tear my shirt enough so she could get the scalpel out. Her hand passed through it, and they both gasped.

Jim, are you there?

**"I'm right here."** Someone squeezed my hand. **"They have it on camera. Someone dressed as a nurse knocked Devin out from behind. Then the intruder stabbed you and connected the device to another one. The hospital is on lockdown. We'll find who did this. I swear it. You're going to be alright."**

Tears pricked my eyes. I can't get out, Jim. What happened? Why can't I leave?

**"I'm plugging into the device as we speak and will search the code."**

I coughed, feeling wet, sticky blood coming out of my mouth. The moon got brighter. There were two of them for some reason. No, wait, they were huge. They resembled car headlights.

**"Gunther?"**

Jim?

My vision swam. People stood right above me. My characters. No, wait. It was too bright a room for a medieval fantasy story. And everyone wore hospital masks. My characters wouldn't wear masks. It was too clean.

**"Gunther!"**

A man appeared in my vision. He wore a three-piece suit surrounded by doctors and nurses with a small headset on. I recognized him. He had a phone in one hand, glancing at it before looking at me. **"Are you coming back to us?"**

Jim. I recognized his voice anywhere. It sounded patched, like I could hear it from my story, but also in real life. I took a deep breath, feeling the sharp pain in my gut as my eyes rolled up to my head. **"Say the code! Say it!!"**

Code 0000. I leave my story.

I slammed back into my world, my characters coming in clearer, trying to talk to me, their voices overlapping.

"No!" My shout was partially in pain, mostly in heartbreak.

**"Alright. We'll get through this."**

The scalpel disappeared from my gut, and I screamed, this time completely in pain.

Roger's jaw dropped. "What happened? What's going on?"

"I don't know." Tears fell down Tara's cheeks as she grabbed the hem of her dress and pressed it against my bleeding wound. "This is some sort of dark magic. It's the only thing that could kill a God."

Jim? What's happening?

**"They've got it out."**

My eyes closed, and anger bubbled to the surface. "I *know*. I felt it! Why can't I leave?"

Roger pulled out a dagger, glancing at Tara, waiting for her permission. He placed the blade near my open wound, where the medical scalpel disappeared. I was still bleeding out. Alwin stood, his arrow pointed right at my eye even as the concern he felt for me was real. Paldric had a hand on my shoulder, keeping me steady. I still felt someone grasping my hand that belonged to none of my characters.

**"I will tell you everything I know. Understand it's not complete. There's a second device hooked to yours, and it's got a count down. It's going to pull you into the next device."**

"No. No, it's too soon. The book can't end. I've still got at least ten thousand words to go." I ignored the fact that my characters could hear me.

**"It's ending the second book prematurely and sucking you into another one. There's a permanent code to keep you from leaving this one."**

"Book three? I can't have a book three. No. No! No trilogy! I can't keep this going!"

**"I'm sorry, but the second you enter book three, you've got to leave."**

Can I leave? Is it programed to let me leave?

**"Since it hasn't started yet, I've deleted as many of Professor Andrews' codes as possible. I assure you. You can leave."**

Milla screamed, and Roger and Paldric turned to see shadow soldiers grabbing the little girl and disappearing into the woods. My blood covered hand reached for her. "No! Milla!"

Roger and Paldric raced after the shadow soldiers. I tried to get up, but a searing pain in my gut kept me down. Tara steadied me as a wave of nausea took me over.

**"Please, Gunther. Prepare to leave."**

I can't leave Milla. Not with another eighty thousand words for him to torture her. Professor Andrews may not be in control of the Dark Wizard, but he still has his orders. He'll still alter her. I can't let him. I won't.

A crazy thought came to me. Someone may have stabbed me in the real world, but that doesn't mean I have to feel it now.

**"You're going insane! Can't you see that?"**

My wound sewed itself back up, and the pain disappeared. Tara gasped, grabbing my wrist. "Wait."

I scrambled to my feet, sensing an arrow aimed right at my eye. I lifted my hand to grab it out of the air, my fist closing around the arrowhead that should have punctured my hand. My gaze turned toward my elf. "I need to keep her safe."

Alwin already had another one notched in his bow. "I wouldn't if I were you."

Tara got to her own feet. "Don't do this! You're over a hundred percent!"

I dropped the arrow, turning away from them. "You can't stop me, Alwin. No one can. No one will."

Tara and Alwin tried to shout at me, but they were already far behind, and I ignored them as I ran faster and faster. One could say I was running at an inhumanly fast rate.

**"Gunther! NO!"**

I shut Jim off. Shut all of them off. I couldn't let that little girl get tortured. I could never live with myself.

It was easy to catch up with Roger and Paldric, and I could have surpassed them, but Roger shoved his shoulder against me, causing me to slide to the ground.

"Stop it!" I was already standing, even though I wasn't positive about how I got to my feet so fast. "I need to save her!"

Paldric jumped onto my back, trying to wrestle me to the ground. Roger pulled out his dagger, stabbing me in the stomach. It was as useless as him trying to stab the Dark Wizard.

In fact, I realized the error in my approach. I pushed Roger away, and he flew far, the trunk of the tree snapping his spine, killing him instantly. Despite his need to kill me, I simply waved a hand and brought him back to life. Killing him right after saving him would be too ruthless. I reached out, forcing the Dark Wizard to cease to exist. Forcing the sun to rise. The goblins to turn on each other. To go after the trolls. Forcing the shadow soldiers to burn up in the sunlight.

"Gunther! Please! You don't want to do this! This isn't who you are! You're not evil!" Paldric said.

I grabbed my main character's throat to stop his speech, glaring at him. My fingers tightened over his skin, and he couldn't breathe.

"Milla needs to be safe. I need to check on her. If you are going to stop me, then I will stop you first."

Part of me knew the extremity of my words made little sense. Maybe they were too harsh, but the other, stronger part of me didn't care. Milla needed to be okay, and I would do everything in my power to keep her safe. Paldric tried to say something, but he couldn't. His eyes rolled up, his lids fluttering. He would die if I didn't stop. It didn't matter, though. Even if I killed him, I could always bring him back to life, just as I had with Roger. I could do whatever I wanted. I was God, now. In fact, it would be easier if he was dead to get him out of my way. Milla needed to be safe.

My fingers squeezed Paldric's throat until his neck snapped.

The Story Continues in Book Three...

# Acknowledgements

As always, I must thank my family. Thank you for understanding how much writing means to me, and thank you for letting me slip away every so often to write. Without your love, support, and willing to share me with my characters, this book would have never been written, and I would be a far more stressed out and depressed individual.

Again, thank you, my fans on Royal Road. Thank you for pointing out plot holes, grammar corrections, character inconstancies. Thank you also for reading, rating, following, favoriting, and even giving me some money while my characters were in a rough draft form. It gave me the boost of confidence every writer needs.

Thank you to Getpremades.com for an awesome cover. And thanks to emach55 who was more than willing to make me two maps so Jimdon could be on there. You are the best!

And a final thank you, of course, goes to the people who I will remember were instrumental in the making of this book while I mindlessly do dishes the next day after hitting the publish button. Know water droplets will have gotten all over my kitchen as I threw my hands up in the air in pure frustration at forgetting what you did. You are the best!

# About the Author

Ellen Taylor enjoys living with her husband and three boys, and also enjoys living in her head. She writes in her spare time, because sometimes she needs to be in control of chaos. Follow her on Facebook or Instagram for updates on future books at Ellen Taylor Books.

# **ALSO BY**

<u>Fiction</u>

I Suck at Titles

The Altered Manuscript

<u>Non-Fiction</u>

Give Me Back My Children

www.ingramcontent.com/pod-product-compliance
Lightning Source LLC
Chambersburg PA
CBHW021230310726
48971CB00006B/1755